PAUL BIEGEL

Virgil Nosegay and the Wellington Boots

Translated by **Patricia Crampton**
Illustrated by **Babs van Wely**

Blackie

Originally published in the Netherlands as
Virgilius van Tuil overwintert bij de mensen
by Uitgeversmaatschappij Holland-Haarlem
First published in Great Britain 1984

British Library Cataloguing in Publication Data
Biegel, Paul
Virgil Nosegay and the wellington boots.
I. Title II. Virgilius van Tuil overwintert
bij de mensen. *English*
839. 3' 1364 [J]   PZ7
ISBN 0-216-91495-7

Blackie & Son Limited
Furnival House, 14/18 High Holborn, London WC1V 6BX

Printed in Great Britain by Bell and Bain Ltd., Glasgow.

Contents

1 The Lost Boots 5
2 Taken Home 9
3 In the Middle of the Night 13
4 On the Moor 17
5 In the Bath 21
6 Cathy is Cross 25
7 Neighbours 29
8 The Swing 33
9 A Surprise 37
10 The Return of an Egg 41
11 Ten Visit Virgil 45
12 Father's Hat 49
13 Twice Times Tables 53
14 An Evening Stroll 57
15 Homecoming 60
16 Whispering 64
17 A Tapping on the Window 67
18 A Bright Dog 70
19 Honey to the Moor 73
20 Freedom! 77
21 Dogs at Play 81
22 An Idea 84
23 The Doctor 88
24 Under Arrest 92
25 At the Police Station 96
26 Interrogation 100
27 In Flight 103
28 The Typewriter 106
29 The Little Cushion 110
30 A Cupboardful 114
31 Peter 118
32 The Boots are Found 121
33 The Ventriloquist 125

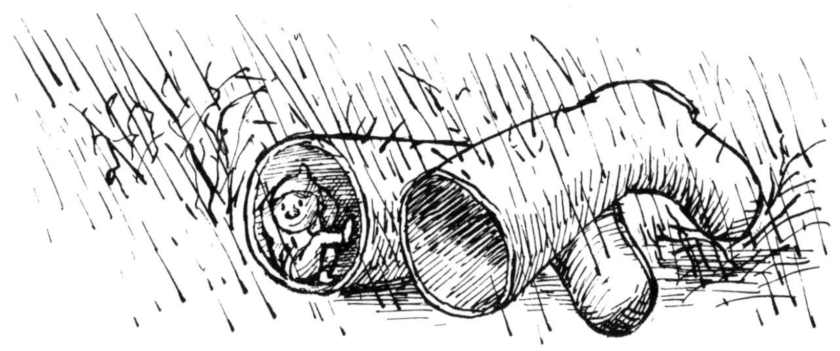

1 The Lost Boots

It rained and it rained and it rained. For days and days and days. It rained on the streets, the pavements, the cars, the people, the grass and the paths. Even the aeroplanes were slithery, slushy, squelchy wet. Even under the big tree the sand had turned to mud. The moor was covered with puddles and the Dwarfs of Nosegay who lived there sat soaked and shivering on the edge of their home in the hollow, for that too had turned into a puddle.

"Not a dry spot anywhere!" they cried, shuddering.

But one of them said: "Except where Virgil is sitting."

"Bah!" cried the others. "Where Virgil is sitting, it smells. And it's a dangerous place. Better to be wet than that."

They sat on, shivering, in silence.

Even the mole tunnels had been flooded.

But Virgil was quite dry. He was the only dry

dwarf on all the moor and he chewed on a grass stalk and watched the rain, leaning comfortably against the curved wall of his hiding-place. Virgil had never felt better.

"What a lot of idiots," he muttered to himself, "sitting out there in the rain while there's plenty of space in here. Well" – he looked behind him into the dark space – "perhaps all hundred of them in here together would be a tight fit. But there's room next door too. I don't understand it."

A mole scurried by and stuck its pink nose inside.

"No," cried Virgil, "be off with you!" He gave the mole's drenched pelt a shove. "Go next door."

Next door – as Virgil called it – were all the others in need of shelter: moths, spiders, two butterflies, a fieldmouse and a millipede.

The mole went. And it rained and rained and went on raining. It rained on all the people, all the umbrellas, all the tiled roofs, all the bicycles. Splash, splash, splash, dashing against the windows.

And behind one of the wet windows of one of the wet houses sat a little boy – as dry as Virgil – staring out. He was alone in the house. His father and his mother and his sister had gone off to the cinema, but he was not allowed to go because his shoes were wet. The little boy's shoes were like sponges and they were standing against the central heating to dry.

"Silly, silly, silly boy," his mother had told him. "How could you lose your boots, your lovely expensive wellington boots – just lose them! And now your shoes are wet, so you'll just have to stay at home."

The little boy had tears in his eyes but he scarcely noticed them because of the rain.

"But where could you have left them?" his father kept on asking. "They didn't grow legs, did they? They must be *somewhere*, those boots of yours?"

That *somewhere* was what the little boy was thinking about now. Somewhere in Japan, or at the North Pole, or on the rubbish tip, or under the sofa. But they were not there.

"What have you done with them then?" his father had asked again.

And his mother had asked an even better question: "When was the last time you were wearing them?"

Wearing them? That was what the little boy was thinking about now. The last time, when was the last time?

And suddenly he knew. It was Sunday a week ago. No, it was Saturday, when they had gone for a walk on the moor.

"On the moor!" the little boy shouted at the weeping window. "That's where I – I wonder if my boots are still there?"

He put on his wet shoes, his wet mackintosh, grabbed his wet bicycle, jumped on the wet saddle and rode splish-splash-splosh to the moor.

They'll have been pinched long ago, he was thinking as he rode. Found long ago. Taken away long ago. Or burned up in a little fire with an awful smell.

He knew exactly where he had taken them off, where the car had been standing when they got back into it.

And that was exactly where they were now. Lying side by side, two wet wellington boots.

"Great!" shouted the little boy. He danced. He pulled off his wet shoes, picked up a boot, lifted one stockinged foot to put it on – and stood stock-still, like a statue, or like a stork standing on one leg.

The boot had shouted: "Don't put it on! It's full up in here!"

The little boy went on standing stock-still for at least a minute. Are they under a spell? he thought. Can my boots suddenly talk? But after a minute such an icy-cold dribble started down his neck from his collar that he quickly took hold of the other boot, turned it upside down and shook it. A lot of odd things rolled out: a mole, a mouse, a millipede, two butterflies, moths and spiders. They disappeared immediately in the heather.

Then the little boy shook out the right boot as well and out rolled Virgil. Virgil, who had shouted: "It's full up in here!" And with that begins a new story about Virgil the dwarf.

2 Taken Home

Virgil tumbled out of the boot onto the wet heather.

"I say!" cried the dwarf. "Can't you be a bit more careful?"

"I er . . ." said the little boy. "I er . . . er, I . . ."

"And I'm getting soaked through as well," cried Virgil. "Haven't you got an umbrella?"

The rain was still pouring down. The little boy's socks were getting wet because he had already taken his shoes off in order to put on his boots. But he could not feel anything. He simply stared, with eyes like saucers.

"Is it really you?" he asked at last.

"Not altogether," said Virgil. "I'm half melted away."

"Er, what did you want?" asked the little boy.

"An umbrella," Virgil shouted again. "Haven't you got one of those big ones? Then the others would be able to get under it too."

"All hundred of them?" said the little boy.

"Yes," said Virgil. "Ha, ha, a sensible human being at last. One who *knows* something."

The little boy had certainly heard of Virgil and of the hundred Dwarfs of Nosegay but naturally he had never believed that they really existed. After all!

"Could I *see* them?" he asked.

"First tell me what your name is," said Virgil.

"Jasper," said the little boy. "Can I see them?"

"First I want to know if you've got one of those umbrellas, Jasper," said Virgil.

"No," said Jasper. "Yes, at home! We've got one at home. A big black one. Can I see them?"

"In your house?" asked Virgil. "Then off you go and get it."

"All right!" cried Jasper. "And then may I – you wait here – oooh, but it's not there. My father and my mother and my sister have taken it with them to the film. But afterwards . . ."

"Oh yes," said Virgil, "*afterwards!* I'll have melted by then. Right away. And the others too. We'll have turned into a puddle, melted by the rain. A snuffling, coughing puddle, because the others have all caught cold. They've been sitting in the wet for days."

Jasper was looking confused. And it went on pouring and pouring and pouring. Jasper was almost beginning to turn into a puddle himself.

"Hey, wait a minute," he cried. "A rubbish bag. I'll get a rubbish bag from home. It's plastic. They'll be dry under that too."

That did sound like a good idea, so Jasper stepped into his boots in order to go straight home, but Virgil shouted: "Stop, wait a minute, what about me?"

"What about you?"

"Well, I was dry in your boot. Now you can take me with you."

Jasper was looking confused again. Then he said: "I'll take you with me then. You'll be dry under my coat."

"Oh . . ." said Virgil. "Oh, all right. As long as you don't squash me."

Jasper picked Virgil up. It was a bit weird having a live dwarf in your hand. What does it feel like? he thought: not like a frog, not like a baby rabbit, not like a fish, not like a puppy . . . Jasper had been allowed to hold a baby once, but it wasn't like that. It's not really like anything else. He popped Virgil into an inside pocket, picked up his shoes, jumped onto his bicycle and rode home.

"I'm stifling!" cried Virgil. "Let me out!"

"We're there now," said Jasper.

He put his bike in the shed and took Virgil out again. "Wait here a moment," he said, setting the dwarf on the workbench among all the tools. "I'll be back right away."

But he was not.

The first thing Jasper saw when he walked into the passage was the umbrella, put out to dry. Back already? he thought. But at that moment his father came rushing out of the living-room, thundering: "Jasper, where have you been?"

Then his mother ran out too, calling: "Jasper! Your boots! Where did you find them?"

And finally his sister had to come and tell him,

sobbing, that the cinema was sold out, that they had not seen the film and that was why they were back so early.

Jasper said: "I've got Virgil with me."

"I want to know where you've been!" his father shouted angrily.

"On the moor," said Jasper. "That's where my boots were. And that's where they are, all hundred of them. Soaking wet in the rain. So I've got to have a rubbish bag. Or the umbrella."

"The moor?" said mother. "Is that where you left your boots?"

"Yes, but I must go now!" cried Jasper. He tried to take the umbrella, but it was no use.

"You'll stay at home," said his father and mother.

"But they're turning into a puddle!" cried Jasper.

"What on earth are you talking about? Have you been dreaming?"

"No!" screamed Jasper. "And if you don't believe me, go and look. In the shed. Virgil is there."

His father and his mother and his sister had heard of the Dwarfs of Nosegay too, of course, but they did not believe they really existed either.

"Well," howled Jasper, because they simply would not let him go, not even out of the room. "You can see him yourselves. He's on the workbench."

"Father," said mother. "Go and have a look."

His father went to the shed. On the workbench there were nails and screws and clamps and lids and pincers and a hardened paintbrush and a drill and an old vacuum cleaner motor.

But no Virgil.

3 In the Middle of the Night

Jasper's father had another good look at the work-bench in the little shed but there was no dwarf among the nails and screws and pincers, nor among the rubbish in the old paint pot.

"I must be mad," father thought to himself. "As if I could believe that a dwarf really existed!"

He went back into the house and said: "No, my boy, there's nothing. You dreamed it."

"I didn't!" cried Jasper. "He was in my boot. He was in my right boot when I found it on the moor. He was sheltering from the rain. And the others weren't. They're melting away now."

"But my boy," said Jasper's mother, "melting? Surely not? That really does sound like a dream: dwarfs that melt in the rain."

But Jasper insisted: "Virgil said it himself."

"Yes," said his father. "Quite right. In your dream, Virgil could have said anything."

Jasper was silent. It was no use talking; they

would never believe him. He looked out of the window at the rain, which simply went on drizzling on and on and on, out of the grey sky. And he thought of the hundred Dwarfs of Nosegay sitting soaked through and slowly turning into a puddle. And of Virgil who – but, he remembered, where could Virgil be? Why had he hidden away? Or – or, Jasper wondered, was it really a dream after all?

"You must dry your boots, my boy," he heard his mother say. "But of course I'm glad you've found them again."

"No," said Jasper.

"No what?"

"It wasn't a dream. Otherwise they wouldn't be wet."

"What's that you're saying?"

But Jasper did not answer. He wiped his boots dry with an old rag, thinking out a plan as he worked.

When he had to go to bed he went obediently to his room, undressed and lay down. But in the dead of night Jasper got out of bed again, dressed himself, crept down to the kitchen, found a plastic rubbish bag, stole down the passage, fell over the umbrella which was still drying out there and went outside. Into the shed. The shed door squeaked terribly loudly in the quiet night, just because Jasper was opening it so carefully.

"Hey, pssst! Virgil!"

No answer.

"Psst! Virgil! Are you there?"

Then he heard a yawn.

"Virgil! Are you asleep? It's me, Jasper!"

The yawn was first yawned right to its very end, then followed by a sigh, then a scratching, then a stirring and a tossing and turning and finally a dwarf's voice which said: "What do you call 'a moment'?"

"What?"

"You said wait here 'a moment'. You'd be back right away. What does right away mean?"

"I couldn't get away," said Jasper. "Where are you now? I can't find the light."

"Here," said Virgil.

Jasper groped his way towards the workbench where there was a torch, but he bumped into the metal sink and it made a loud *boing* in the night. Then he searched among the pots and pincers, found the torch, switched it on and shone it around.

"Where?" he asked unhappily.

"Here, stupid," said Virgil. "In the cat basket under the workbench."

"Why didn't you say so?" said Jasper, pointing the light at the dwarf.

"Were you there earlier on, when my father came in? Why were you hiding? Were you frightened?"

"Frightened?" said Virgil. "What sort of a word is that? And I never saw your father. I think I was already asleep. And stop shining that in my eyes."

"If you had shown yourself to my father," said Jasper, "they would have believed everything. And I would have been able to go back to the moor straight away with a plastic bag for the others to shelter under."

"I was asleep," said Virgil.

"But I've got one now," said Jasper. "A rubbish bag. Are you coming?"

"Coming?" asked Virgil. "Coming where?"

"To the moor. To the others."

"Now?" cried the dwarf. "In the middle of the night?"

"But they'll melt if we don't!" said Jasper. "It's still raining."

"Oh rubbish! Dwarfs don't melt that easily."

"That's what you said!"

"Oh no, I didn't!" There was another yawn. "That was a joke. Go to sleep."

But Jasper was wide awake and resolute. He wanted to see the hundred dwarfs sitting on the edge of their hollow, in the middle of the moor, and to give them a plastic bag to shelter under. "Come on!"

"I'm much too comfortable here," said Virgil. You go alone, since you're so keen."

"Alone?" said Jasper. "I don't know where they are, do I? So I can't find them, can I?"

"Oh, I'll tell you that," said Virgil. "Up the gravel path, then left, then right at the fourth pine tree, and then on a bit. You'll find them there. And say hallo to them from me. Goodbye!" He turned over in the cat basket and went on snoring.

Jasper turned round too. He was not going to let himself be put off. He got his bike, took the plastic bag, jumped into the saddle and rode away.

The moor was quite a long way, the night was very dark, the rain was awfully wet. *And* there was someone who had heard the sink go *boing* and seen the flickering light inside the shed . . . .

4 On the Moor

Jasper bicycled through the dark night and the rain spattered down. But he did not care: he must get to the moor, because now he knew the place where the hundred Dwarfs of Nosegay lived. And with his bicycle lamp and his pocket torch together he would surely be able to find them in the darkness.

Jasper turned on to the gravel path. The pine trees were like dark ghosts with arms that waved in the passing light of his bicycle lamp.

At the end of the path he turned left. It was narrower here and the ghosts were closer in.

After the fourth ghost Jasper had to turn right and then on a bit. He got off his bike, put it down on the heather, and walked on by the light of his pocket torch.

"The hollow," he muttered to himself. "The hollow must be just up here."

The ghostly arms swayed and struck him in the face with wet pine-needle fingers. But Jasper must and would see the dwarfs, all hundred of them, and he shone his torch over the ground from left to right across the heather. And yes, there was a hollow, half full of water, and round the edge of the hollow, shivering and shuddering and soaking, squelching wet, sat a hundred . . .

But at that moment a harsh voice barked out behind him: "Now, now, what's going on here?"

Jasper got such a terrible fright that he dropped the torch. A ghost, he thought.

But it was a perfectly ordinary policeman and he had a torch too, and he inspected Jasper with it from top to toe.

"What is a little boy like you doing on the moor in the middle of the night?" he wanted to know.

"Nothing, sir," said Jasper.

"I saw you," said the policeman. "First in the shed (that was where the sound of the sink and the flickering light of Jasper's torch had attracted his attention) and after that I followed you here. What mischief are you up to?"

"Mischief?" asked Jasper.

"Speak up now."

"Well," said Jasper then, "looking for dwarfs."

"Looking for dwarfs, eh? What kind of game is that?"

"Game? It's true, sir."

"Oh yes? Where are they then?"

"Here, in the hollow." Jasper picked up his torch. He shone it on the hollow and round the edge. "Here they are," he said, "all hundred of them."

But not a single dwarf was there.

"In the water, are they?" asked the policeman.

"No," said Jasper, almost crying. "You frightened them away."

"I think so too," said the policeman. "Now you come along with me. I'm going to take you home."

But Jasper put the plastic bag down beside the hollow. "Here you are!" he cried. "Here you are, Nosegay Dwarfs. You can shelter under that. And Virgil says hallo!"

The policeman wanted to know what he was talking about, so Jasper said: "Oh that was just my little game," and walked obediently back to his bicycle. The policeman had put his bicycle down in the same place and together they rode home again.

"This is where I live," said Jasper. "Goodbye, sir."

But it was no use. The policeman came with him and rang the doorbell three times, before Jasper's father and mother woke up. And oh dear, oh dear, what a to-do there was then.

"Now all this dwarf rubbish is really too much," said Jasper's mother.

"But I saw them sitting there!" cried Jasper. "In the hollow, and then – Virgil is asleep in the shed!"

"But, my boy," said his mother. "Your father went and looked there, didn't he?"

"He's in the cat basket," cried Jasper. "Under the workbench."

The policeman said: "Might I perhaps be allowed to know who this Virgil is?"

"Oh, look, Officer," said father, "he's a dwarf in a story. But Jasper thinks he really exists."

"I *see*," said the policeman. "In a story – now I begin to understand."

Jasper was getting furious. "Go and have a look!" he yelled.

But father and mother were in their night clothes and had no desire to go out to the shed in all the wet; they made coffee for the policeman, who sat slurping it down on a chair, with his cap off. Suddenly he was an ordinary man in a policeman's uniform, instead of a real policeman.

"Thank you," he said, when the cup was empty. "I'll be off, then."

Jasper had to go to bed, but his bicycle was still outside and he would have to put it in the shed. The policeman gave him a hand. "Then I can take a look at this Virgil, at the same time," he said.

He was wearing his cap again. He lit the way with his bright police lamp and from under the work-bench came a yawn. Then another. And then came a voice from under the bench: "Are you there at last? Did you find them? And did they say anything?"

The policeman pointed the light at the cat basket. And with his own eyes he saw the dwarf. A luxuriously lounging, widely yawning dwarf.

5 In the Bath

Virgil was woken up by the bright light from the policeman's lamp.

"Turn it out!" he shouted. "It hurts my eyes."

The policeman scratched his head. "I observe," he said, "I observe a dwarf."

And Jasper, who had put his bike down, cried: "Do you see, do you see, do you see? Do you see that he's real?"

"Ah, well," said the policeman, "but first a closer investigation . . ."

"Look here," cried Virgil, "turn that tiresome light off. And shut your mouth. I want to sleep."

But Jasper said: "Please Virgil, come along now. Come in and see my father and mother. They don't believe in you."

"Tomorrow morning," said Virgil with a yawn.

"No, now!" shouted Jasper. He stooped to pick Virgil up, but his shadow stooped with him and made everything black under the workbench.

Jasper groped round the cat basket, but the cushions were empty.

"Virgil!" he shouted. His hand groped further across the floor. The policeman shone his torch from the side but the dwarf was nowhere to be seen.

"Well, boy, he's gone," said the policeman. "I observe no dwarf."

Jasper was very unhappy. "But you *did* see him," he cried. "Please tell my father and mother, tell them that you saw him."

"Hm, yes," said the policeman, "hm, yes, perhaps it was an effect of the shadow, a trick of the light."

"Virgil!" cried Jasper. "Where have you got to now?"

But the walls of the shed remained silent, there was not even a creak or a squeak to be heard.

"But you *heard* him too," said Jasper. "You heard him talking!"

"Hm, yes," said the policeman, "hm, yes, perhaps, but with the trickling and pattering of the rain on the roof . . ."

Jasper realized that the policeman did not want to tell his parents anything. No, the policeman simply went away, on his bicycle, and Jasper went into the house and to bed, without saying anything. Angry, sorrowful and unhappy.

And Virgil?

He was muttering to himself. And he was angry and sorrowful and unhappy too. "All this disturbance! Why can they never leave a dwarf in peace?"

Virgil had jumped out of the cat basket when

Jasper bent down, and crept away under a pile of wood, but now he had found a new place in a box of screws and nuts and washers and an old oilcan. And he had found a rag which he could use as a coverlet.

"It does stink of grease," he grumbled, "and the other one was stinking of the cat." But at least he was indoors and dry.

Next morning when Jasper had to go to school he took another look round in the shed, but of course he did not think of looking in the little box. And after school he bicycled off to the moor to look for the dwarfs, by the hollow where he had taken the plastic bag the night before. But by day the moor looked quite different from in the darkness by lamplight. There were no ghosts with waving arms, all the paths looked quite ordinary and the hollow was nowhere to be found. Nor was the plastic bag. And it was not raining any more. Jasper suddenly understood that there were two worlds – one world by day and one world by night. They were quite different, and your thoughts were different in each world, as well. Day-thoughts and night-thoughts. And day-thinking, he bicycled home again.

But at home, Jasper's mother had been looking for a screw. It was for the foot of the lamp, because it had always been loose and she had decided to fix it at last with a strong screw that fitted. So she carried the whole box with all the screws in it out of the shed, in order to try them one by one until she found the right one.

Jasper's mother sat down comfortably beside the lamp and opened the box.

"Oh, hallo," said Virgil. "I thought you were Jasper."

"No, I'm not Jasper. I'm Jasper's mo . . ." Then she stopped. Her mouth fell open, her eyes bulged, and as Virgil got to his feet in the box she cried: "What do you look like! In all that grease and oil, ugh! Who on earth would go and sleep under a dirty rag in a toolbox like that, yuk!"

Virgil had never come across anything like this before. He could not get a word out.

"You're going straight into the bath," said Jasper's mother. "And you'll wash your own clothes. Come on!"

That was the reason why, when Jasper came home and called, "Hallo Mum!" and went to his room to put on another jersey, he saw Virgil sitting there in the washbasin, half covered with water and foam. Virgil in the nude, snorting and splashing, busy getting himself and his clothes clean.

"Eyes front!" shouted the dwarf.

6 Cathy is Cross

"Mum!" called Jasper. "Mum, Mum! The dwarf is in the bath, in my basin, in the bath in my basin, in my . . ." Jasper was thoroughly over-excited. He rushed into the living-room. "In my room!" he shouted. "With soap and foam and no clothes on, I mean he's washing himself."

"Yes, my boy," said his mother calmly. "I know."

"You *know?!*"

"I put him there myself," she said. "He looked filthy. Under that oil."

"But . . . but that's Virgil!" cried Jasper.

"Yes, my boy, of course it's Virgil."

"But, but . . ." Suddenly Jasper was furious: "First you wouldn't believe it," he shouted, "and NOW . . ."

"Now I can *see* it," said his mother, cool as a cucumber. "That's quite different."

Well! Jasper was speechless.

And then his sister Cathy came home. She was

going to her ballet class later, she had the right dress and shoes for it. She wanted to go and put them on right away and jump around in them, as she usually did, but Jasper cried: "Virgil is in my washbasin!"

"What?" she said.

"Virgil. Now you can *see* that he's real. Come on!"

Cathy made such a face that she looked like a photograph on the fold of a newspaper. "Mum," she said, "what's up with Jasper? Has he fallen on his head?"

"No, my child," said their mother. "At least, not as far as I know. You just go with him and have a look."

Cathy's face slowly straightened out again.

"Although . . ." Mother went on. "Just wait a minute. Virgil won't like it if we come and look at him while he's in the bath."

"Oh phooey!" said Cathy. "That's a good joke! Ha, ha, ha, I'm not going to fall for that."

"You don't have to," said her mother. "You'll be seeing it."

"Yes!" cried Jasper, who was angry again now. "You certainly will see it. I'm going to bring Virgil down right away. Then you can have a good look at him with your own eyes, and then I shall tell him to pinch your nose, really hard, and you'll be able to feel him too."

"Huh, you!" said Cathy. "Get away." She left the room and went up to put on her ballet things. But, well, Cathy was just a little bit curious after all, so she did, very cautiously, open Jasper's door and peep round the corner at the basin. Then she gave a shout and ran down the stairs again into the living-room. "How mean!" she shouted. "How mean, what a mean trick!"

"But my dear child, whatever is the matter?" asked her mother.

"My dolls' clothes! He's taken my dolls' clothes and put them in the water. Meanie!"

"Me?" gasped Jasper.

"Dolls' clothes?" said Mother.

They went to look.

The wash basin in Jasper's room was half full of water. A little foam was still drifting about on top, grey-brown in colour, and laundry was soaking in it. Tiny bits of laundry.

"Oh, my dear child, those are not your dolls' clothes at all, can't you see? Those are Virgil's clothes." Mother wrang them out one by one and hung them up to dry.

But Cathy stamped her foot. "They are!" she shouted. "Of course they are!"

She had not played with her dolls for a long time now, so perhaps she no longer remembered, or perhaps she did not want to see that the clothes were different. She thought it was a rotten joke, an unkind joke, about the dwarf, and she thought they ought to stop right now.

"Where is he then?" she cried, weeping tears of anger. "Well, where is he? That Virgil?"

And when there was no answer she turned on her heel and left the room, slamming the door behind her. There! She was cross.

Mother followed her out. So Jasper was left alone

in his room and he heard a deep sigh. It came from under the bed where his towel had been stuffed, or rather rolled up, with Virgil in the middle.

"What a row there is in this human house," said Virgil. "Is it always like this?"

"No," said Jasper. "You must let them see you. Then they won't have to carry on like that."

"I don't just let people see me," said Virgil. "And certainly not when I'm coming out of the bath."

"Really," said Jasper impatiently. "Why did you have to have a bath?"

"Your mother said I must," said Virgil.

"Well, all right," said Jasper. "Can I call my sister now?"

"Are you crazy?" said Virgil. "I'm not dressed."

"You've got that towel round you, haven't you?"

"I want my clothes. And they'll have to be dry."

Jasper fetched the drier from the bathroom and blew into the dwarf's wet shirt and trousers with it so that they puffed up and steamed themselves dry.

"Here you are," he said.

"Turn round," said Virgil.

"Hurry up," said Jasper.

"Ready!" called Virgil.

Jasper went to the door, opened it and called: "Cathy, come and have a look, he's here!"

But Cathy was cross. She was in a huff and she was going to stay in it. She did not come to look.

"Leave it, Jasper," said Virgil. "She'll come round. There's plenty of time, because I'm going to tell you something: I'm planning to live here for a while. I think it's very nice to be in a human house."

7 Neighbours

So Virgil decided to stay for a time in the house with the human beings.

Jasper was in the know and so was his mother. But his father was not, he thought it was all nonsense. And Cathy would have nothing at all to do with it; she wasn't going to be made a fool of.

Virgil did not care a bit. What he minded about was not the people but the house, and in the mornings it was nice and empty: the children were at school, father and mother at work, and he could have a nice game playing about with the lid of the breadbin. He ran down the passage as fast as he could go and slid the last bit across the smooth tiles on his trousered bottom. He sent a couple of empty bottles rolling across the kitchen tiles, clash, clash into each other, and then the front door bell rang.

Virgil was quiet for a moment. Then he shouted: "Not at home!"

At once the bell rang again. Louder and longer.

"I told you," shouted Virgil from behind the door, "there's nobody at home. The people are not here!"

"Who are you then?" said a voice.

"Me?" shouted Virgil. "That's none of your business. Goodbye!" Once again he took a run down the passage and slid with a bump into the lavatory door.

"People," he muttered to himself. "Human beings always want to *know* everything. Who are you? What are you doing there? And when you tell them they don't believe you. Then they say: there's no such thing as a dwarf."

Well, Virgil was right: a little later there was not only another ring at the door, somebody was knocking on it too. Very hard. And a man's voice was calling: "Who's that in the house?"

Virgil put on his deepest voice and growled: "The giant Brobdingnag!" Because he had heard the children's mother reading them a story about a giant with that name.

There was a rattling at the front door and a whisper of voices: "Have we got to fetch the police?"

"Yes!" said Virgil. "Do!"

He had managed to wriggle open the cupboard in the passage: the vacuum cleaner was in there. Virgil unwound the flex and pushed the plug very carefully into the wall contact, and when a voice shouted from outside the door: "If you don't open the door this minute – "

Virgil switched on the vacuum cleaner so that it began to roar and drowned the man's words. Then he switched it off again and shouted in his giant's voice: "Did you hear my dragon? You'd better watch out, or he'll blow fire through the letterbox!"

There must have been at least ten people on the pavement when the children's mother came home at lunchtime. "Mrs Hood," they said. "There are squatters in your house."

"Oh no!" said mother. "Squatters?"

"They're making a noise and they won't open the door," said the neighbours.

"Ah," said mother. "I think that's Virgil."

"Virgil?" they enquired, very, very inquisitive now. "Who's that? A lodger?"

"Yes," said mother.

"Well, he's a very naughty, noisy one. Family, I suppose?"

"No," said mother. "Just a dwarf. Let me pass please, I can't get the key into the door."

The neighbours moved aside but crowded in again at once as soon as the door was open, because they were so curious to catch a glimpse of . . . of whom, exactly? What mysterious things were going on in that house, they wanted to know. A dwarf! Must be something pretty bad if you had to think up a story like that.

But once inside mother said: "Virgil, you mustn't make such a noise, nor such a mess. The neighbours don't like it."

She rolled the vacuum cleaner flex up again, put the bottles to rights, popped Virgil on the work counter and made him help to shape the meat balls. Little ones, to go in the soup. He could do that. "What would I do without you?" said mother.

But outside there was someone peering through

the window. It was the most inquisitive of all the neighbours, Mr Walker from across the way, an old man with rickety knees and deaf ears, but eyes which were still sharp, and he was using them to stare and stare, until mother saw him there.

"What is this, Mr Walker?" she cried, opening the back door. "What are you doing here?"

"What did you say?" he said. "I'm short of an egg. Can you lend me one?"

But he was staring at Virgil, who was now stooping, as if turned to stone, over a meat ball.

"An egg?" said Mother. "Is that what you've come for?"

She took one from the cupboard and gave it to him. "There you are. Goodbye, Mr Walker."

"What did you say?"

But mother had already closed the back door and Mr Walker hobbled out of the garden on his ramshackle legs. But he had seen Virgil. Living and moving. And by the gate he bumped into Cathy.

8 The Swing

"Good morning, Mr Walker," said Cathy, when she saw Mr Walker at the gate.

But Mr Walker shouted: "I tell you, I saw him. With my very own eyes. And I'm going to do something about it."

"What do you mean, Mr Walker?"

"What did you say?"

"What do you mean?"

"What do I mean? The dwarf, of course."

Cathy looked at him and began to get cross. "You too?" she cried.

"Me too?" cried Mr Walker. "The whole neighbourhood came out. Everyone was standing in front of your door."

"What?" said Cathy.

"But I saw him, I saw the dwarf. And it won't do. It's not right. It's dangerous. He was rolling meat balls in your kitchen. I wouldn't eat them if I were you. Good-day to you."

Mr Walker hobbled home to his house on the opposite side of the road and Cathy ran indoors. "Mum!" she called.

"Hallo dear," said her mother, who was just coming downstairs. "Come into the kitchen. I'm busy in there."

Cathy went into the kitchen. There were meat balls lying on the breadboard by the sink, but there was no sign of any dwarf rolling them.

"There you are," said Cathy.

"Where are you?" asked her mother.

"Oh, nothing. Mr Walker is crazy."

"No he's not," said her mother. "He's just inquisitive. He saw Virgil, didn't he? Did he tell you? I suppose you've just bumped into him?"

But Cathy had already left the kitchen and she was furious, absolutely furious because she was still being made a fool of, and now apparently the whole neighbourhood was taking part. Mr Walker! And he was going to 'do something about it' – pah!

Cathy went up to her room and slammed the door behind her – crash! She was very cross.

There was a bed in Cathy's room and a cupboard and a table with a drawer and a chair. The chair had been pushed back and something was swinging from the knob of the drawer. One of Cathy's ballet shoes was hanging there from its long silk ribbons and swinging to and fro: under the table, away from the table, under the table again, out again, in again – and it went on and on swinging, as steadily as a garden swing. At first Cathy thought it was caused by the draught from the slamming door, but the slipper went on swinging: under the table, out again, under the . . . Is there a mouse in there? Cathy wondered, but then she understood. Suddenly she understood quite horribly clearly and even while she was unable to believe that she believed it, she found herself speaking: "I say," she said, "is that you, Virgil?"

"Yes, of course," came the answer from the swinging shoe. "And give me a little push, would you? I want to go higher."

Cathy did so, with one finger.

"Hey, not as idiotically high as all that!" cried Virgil. "I don't want to bump my head."

Cathy stopped the slipper, untied the ribbons and put it on the table. "Now I want to look at you," she said.

Virgil scrambled out of the toe and made a bow.

"Gosh," said Cathy. And then she said, "Gosh" again, because it really is quite a special moment when you see Virgil for the first time.

"Can you sneeze, too?" asked Cathy.

"Oh yes," said Virgil. "But not now."

"Oh," said Cathy. She looked and looked. "I thought you were just a fairy tale," she said.

"Oh," said Virgil. He was looking too. Cathy's face was really very sweet.

"But then," Cathy began, "if you're not a fairy story, if you're real, then you have to eat and sleep and go outside from time to time as well. Just like a kitten."

"Yes, of course," said Virgil.

"Do you go through the cat door then?" she

asked. “That flap over the hole that father sawed in the back door?”

“Yes, of course,” said Virgil again.

“That was for our cat,” said Cathy. “She’s dead, but now we’ve got a dwarf. Gosh!” She was beginning to turn quite red in the face. Then she said suddenly: “But you must watch out for the neighbour’s dog when it goes outside. It’s a horrid dog. A dangerous brute. It bites. Its name is Cinders. It’s a girl dog.”

“Oh,” said Virgil. “You needn’t worry about me, you know.”

Father simply would not believe that the dwarf was there. Absolutely not. They were sitting round the table and Cathy had told them everything. “And he’s up in my room,” she said. “Now. Swinging in my slipper.”

But father obstinately refused to go and look. “Oh yes, yes,” he said, “just so that you can laugh at me. I wouldn’t dream of it.”

“I know,” said Jasper suddenly. And he whispered something in his mother’s ear and then in Cathy’s ear.

9 A Surprise

Jasper's plan was this. If father really would not believe that Virgil existed, Jasper was going to make sure that he *saw* Virgil.

It was going to be father's birthday that very week, and he would be getting presents – a whole basketful – and that was what gave Jasper his idea.

"Virgil," he said, on the evening before the birthday, in his bedroom, "Virgil . . . I say, where are you now?"

Virgil was in the folds of the curtains.

"Listen," said Jasper, "you've got to help me."

"With sums?" asked Virgil. "I don't feel like it."

"No," said Jasper. "And not with geography either. With a poem."

"What's that?" asked Virgil.

"Something that rhymes," said Jasper. "JASPER IS A GASPER, for instance, that's what they always say to me at school. It rhymes, but it's nonsense."

"Oh," said Virgil, "what rhymes with me?"

"A cup of tea," said Jasper immediately.

"No," cried Virgil impatiently, "I mean what rhymes with *me,* with Virgil, of course."

"With Virgil?" said Jasper. "Virgil – can't think of anything. I suppose you could say: 'Vir*gil* was ill, so he took a pill'."

"Is that a poem?" asked the dwarf.

"It certainly is," said Jasper. "And a very good one."

"Right," said Virgil. "Have we finished, then?"

"Finished?"

"You had to make a poem, didn't you?"

"Oh yes, but that's different. Quite different. Listen."

And Jasper told Virgil about the birthday and the basketful of presents and his plan to put one extra parcel with them, just a little one, as a surprise.

"Who for?" asked Virgil.

Jasper told him his plan.

"Hurrumph," said Virgil. "Hurrumph, umph . . . All right then."

He said no more.

They had the birthday tea-party next day. Father, mother, Cathy and Jasper sat round the table that evening, with the teapot on one side, a plate of chocolate biscuits on the other and the basket of presents beside the table.

"Well," said father, "now you've sung *Happy Birthday,* I can begin opening my presents!"

First, one from Jasper: a woolly cap for winter walks on the moor. Then from Cathy: some playing cards with a pretty picture on the back. Then a book from mother: it looked very dull. Then another from Jasper: a box.

"No!" cried Jasper. "Don't hold it upside down!"

Father was holding the wrapped box in his hand.

"*This way up*, it says," cried Jasper breathlessly. "Do be careful!"

Father unwrapped the box, taking the paper off carefully, because the top had to stay on top, and there, on the lid of the box, he found a poem.

Father read:

It's true, it's true, it's true!
If father only knew.
But father only knows
What's under the end of his nose.
I tell you in verse
He can't see a gnome,
And what's even worse
It's in his own home.
So pull up your socks
And look in the box.
Be careful, don't spill!
You won't find a pill
And what's better still
You'll discover Vir . . .

"Gil!" shouted the box, and the lid flew off before father could lift it. And *atishoo!* came from the open box.

"Oooh!" cried Cathy. "Now you have really sneezed!"

"There's a lot of dust in that box," said mother.

But father said nothing. He just stared. He stared and stared. Nobody spoke. Even the teapot stopped steaming. Then at last father said: "Hallo, Virgil. You are real, I see." And with his finger and thumb, very, very carefully, Father lifted the little dwarf out of the box.

"Now you see," said Jasper breathlessly. "Now you can really see, Dad."

"Dad?" cried Virgil, walking across the table. "Dad, that rhymes with glad. And I'll be glad if you'll give me a biscuit."

Mother gave him one, broken into little bits, so that he could eat it easily. But just as he was sitting down he saw something move. Outside, at the window, through a gap in the curtains, he saw a face move. Virgil said nothing.

10 The Return of an Egg

No, Virgil did not say whom he had seen staring through the window, but on Boxing Day there was a very loud ring at Jasper's doorbell.

"There must be an elephant at the door," said mother. "Do go and have a look."

Jasper ran to the door. There was no sign of a trunk sticking through the letterbox, but he shouted: "Good morning Mr Elephant," and opened the door.

There was Mr Walker from opposite, with a hand held to his deaf ear. "Whassay?" he said. "What was that you said?"

"I said: 'Good morning Mr Walker'!" shouted Jasper.

"Oh," said Mr Walker. "I came to return an egg to your mother. I borrowed it."

"Oh," said Jasper.

"Is she in?" asked Mr Walker.

"I'll just go and ask," said Jasper, and turning

away from the door he called towards the living-room: "Mum, are you in?"

"No!" shouted mum. "I'm out!"

"Did you hear that?" asked Jasper. "My mother is out. You can give me the egg and I'll give it to mum when she comes back."

Mr Walker was just going to turn away when Jasper's mother came in to the passage. "That was just a joke, Mr Walker," she cried.

"Whassay?"

"A joke! What did you want?"

"Yes," said Mr Walker.

"He's brought you back an egg, Mum," said Jasper.

"The egg? Oh, did you want to see Virgil?"

"Whassay?"

"Virgil!" yelled mother.

Then another voice came from inside the house: "Here!" cried the voice. "I'm in the kitchen." It was Virgil himself, thinking that someone had been calling him.

"No," said Mr Walker. "An egg, I borrowed it."

"Yes," said Mother. "When you came to stare at our dwarf. And you've come to do the same thing now, haven't you?"

"Whassay?"

It really did seem as if Mr Walker was only deaf when he didn't want to hear something.

"Wait a minute," said Jasper. He went to the kitchen, picked Virgil up, sat him on his shoulder and came back to the front door. "Here he is, Mr Walker." And to the dwarf he said: "Virgil, this is

Mr Walker from opposite."

"I know," said Virgil.

"Oh yes?" said Mr Walker, filled with suspicion.

"You were staring the other night," shouted the dwarf. "You were staring in through the window while we were opening the presents."

"Is that true?" asked Jasper's mother.

"Whassay?" said Mr Walker.

"You heard perfectly well!" shouted Jasper, but Mr Walker put up his hand and pointed at the dwarf with his thick forefinger: "It won't do," he began, in a rasping voice. "It's got to get out of our neighbourhood. Dwarfs – they don't exist – and if they do exist they're dangerous. He's got to go."

"But Mr Walker," said mother. "What nonsense is this?"

And Jasper got absolutely furious. He wanted to attack Mr Walker, kick him and bash him with feet and fists, and scratch him too, perhaps. But before he could get started there was a tug at his ear. It was Virgil. And then Virgil began to laugh. He laughed very loud and cried, in his high clear voice, "Hee hee hee! That Mr Walker! *He* doesn't exist. He's just a bit of make-believe. Mr Walker is make-believe!"

"Whassay?"

But then mother and Jasper began to laugh too, and Mr Walker hated it so much that he suddenly turned on his heel and walked off in a rage. At the gate he fished in his coat pocket, brought out something and threw it, in a fury, against the front door.

Mother had just closed the door, and that was lucky, because what Mr Walker had thrown was the egg. The borrowed egg, which he had come to return and had not given back.

"There!" he screamed. The blobs of egg ran slowly down the door to the ground.

"What a nasty man," said Virgil. "Perhaps I'd better go after all?"

"No!" cried Jasper.

And Jasper's mother said: "Virgil, you don't have to run away from our neighbour opposite."

So Virgil stayed. In the house of the human beings, where he was very comfortable. But that evening Jasper said: "Look Virgil, would you like to go to the moor tomorrow and show me the hollow? I really would love to see the others properly just once, the hundred Dwarfs of Nosegay."

"Well, let's go," said Virgil.

11 Ten Visit Virgil

The next afternoon Jasper took the dwarf and his bike and rode off to the moor. "You'll have to show me the way," he said.

"Straight on," said Virgil. "Stop, not so fast. Left here. And now right."

Jasper rode on.

"And this is where you turn off," said Virgil.

Jasper braked. "Where?" he asked. "There's no path here at all."

"Well, pooh," said Virgil, "did you think that we dwarfs lived just off the bicycle track? On some nice, numbered path?"

"No," said Jasper. "No, of courst not." He got off, put his bike down and began to walk in the direction where Virgil was pointing.

Am I really going to see them now, he thought, really, by day, in their hollow? For the last time Jasper had been quite unable to find in daylight the place where he had been at night. The dark moor with its ghostly pines was quite different from the everyday moor. And it was on the ordinary everyday moor that Jasper was going to see the hollow . . .

"Quiet," said Virgil. "Stand still now. And look carefully behind that little birch tree – oh no, it's a mountain ash, I'm wrong, we have to go on a bit."

Jasper walked on, right across the tussocks of heather where you could easily twist your ankle.

"There," said Virgil, "that little tree, that's the one, behind there. Put me down and wait till I call."

Jasper put Virgil down and waited for him to call.

"Come on! They're not here!" called Virgil.

But when Jasper came round the little birch tree he could see the plastic bag which he had taken there that night as a shelter against the rain. The plastic bag had been hung up, stretched like a circus tent above a hollow in the moor. That *must* be the hollow of the hundred dwarfs. Jasper knelt down and stared in all directions but there was not a single dwarf to be seen – except of course for Virgil.

"In winter they live in a mole tunnel," said Virgil. "I just didn't think of that. I'll go and call them."

He strode away through the tall tussocks of heather and Jasper waited. And waited and waited.

And in Jasper's house they were waiting too. Ten of them.

It was Mr Walker from opposite who had taken care of that. For he planned to get even with the dwarf. He was going to do something about it, as he had said. He had gone to the neighbours – the neighbours on the left and the neighbours on the right, and the neighbours of the neighbours on the left, and the neighbours of the neighbours on the right, and the neighbours of the neighbours of the neighbours, and the neighbours behind and the neighbours opposite. Mr Walker had been ringing doorbells everywhere and saying: "They've got a dwarf living in Jasper's house, and it won't do."

"Oh, Mr Walker, you must be mistaken," said one neighbour. And another: "Did you say a dwarf? What sort of rubbish is that?" And a third: "I suppose you dreamed it?" And a fourth, a lady called Mrs Stonehouse-Dashwood, said: "So what?"

But the fifth said: "A dwarf? Goodness gracious, this I have to see," and he went along with Mr Walker to the sixth neighbour, and cried: "There's a dwarf in Jasper's house, a real one, Mr Walker has seen it himself, come and have a look."

And the seventh and the eighth and the ninth and the tenth neighbours all went to have a look. When the first and the second and the third saw them, they all ran out of their houses to follow the others – except for Mrs Stonehouse-Dashwood, who gave piano lessons and did not hold with gaping and gossiping. "No no," she cried, "third finger on F sharp," and she was quite right.

Then the bell rang at Jasper's house, and there they were at the front door, all ten of them: ten neighbours, minus Mrs Stonehouse-Dashwood makes nine, plus Mr Walker makes ten again.

"Well, well," said Jasper's mother as she opened the door. "Is something going on? Can it be my birthday?"

"No," they cried. "We want to see the dwarf."

"Oh naturally," said mother. "Do come in." And she called: "Virgil, where are you? Visitors for you!"

But Virgil was not there. Of course he wasn't. He was on the moor with Jasper. And Jasper's mother searched from the attic to the cellar, taking a special look in Cathy's ballet slippers.

"We'll wait," said the neighbours. But some of them began to look sideways at Mr Walker. Was this all a joke, and was Jasper's mother playing it too?

"It's really too silly of us to believe it," they were beginning to say, "a dwarf . . ."

But then – then Jasper came storming in, breathless, from the moor. "Mum!" he shouted, "Mum, I saw all hundred of them, all the hundred Dwarfs of Nosegay!"

For a moment there was dead silence.

Then his mother said: "Did you, my boy? Then where is Virgil?"

"Here," said Jasper. "In my coat pocket. He showed them to me. They all came out, out of a mole hill, in the middle of the moor, where they live in wintertime, and they had been using my plastic bag against the rain, like a tent, and they said thank you to me, and then they asked Virgil – Virgil – Vir . . . What?"

Jasper stopped, bewildered. His coat pocket was empty. The dwarf was no longer there.

12 Father's Hat

The ten neighbours were sitting in a circle and Jasper was standing in the middle. "He was here," he cried, still panting from bicycling so fast. "In my coat pocket."

They stared at him. Then one of them said: "Oh yes, tell that to the cat."

And another said: "Pull the other one."

And a third: "Teach your grandmother to suck eggs."

And then they all burst out: "Making fools of us! A dwarf in the house, ha, ha. And a hundred on the moor. Ha, ha, ha, ha!" They were angry.

And they all turned on Mr Walker. "It was you that told us!" they cried. "You started it. What a lot of twaddle! But we're not going to be caught again."

Mr Walker heard all this quite well with his deaf ears. He swallowed and said: "But I saw him myself. With my own eyes. He was sitting on the boy's shoulder. A real, live dwarf."

"Oh yes, you're as blind as you're deaf, aren't you? Was it one dwarf or a hundred?"

There was a row. Jasper's mother told them they must go and fight it out in the street and she pushed the ten neighbours out of the door one by one. You could still hear fragments of a sentence here and there:

" . . . I've always said he was half bats . . ."

"Scandal is the only thing he . . ."

" . . . the boy's not much better . . ."

"That mother of his . . ."

The last person to be pushed out of the door by that mother of his was Mr Walker himself.

"Goodbye!"

Mother closed the door firmly behind him. "Jasper," she said, "Jasper, where have you left Virgil?"

"I don't know, Mum," said Jasper, half crying. "Lost him on the way. He was in my coat pocket."

"Not at all."

"What do you mean, not at all?"

"Not lost."

"Not . . .?" Jasper and his mother both fell silent. And both of them looked towards the coat rack. For that was where the voice had come from, the voice that had also shouted 'goodbye' just now, and 'not at all' and 'not lost.'

Virgil, of course.

The dwarf was in father's old hat. It was left hanging on the coat rack and was never worn.

"Is that where you are?" asked Jasper.

"No," called Virgil, "I'm in the cellar."

"Why?" asked Jasper, "why did you . . ."

"Well, I mean," said Virgil, "did you think that I wanted to be displayed to all those people? To ten neighbours? Pah! When you came into the house I just jumped across – from your pocket onto the coat and then up to the hat. Nice and safe."

"Yes," said Jasper, "and I looked like an idiot." He picked up the hat where Virgil was lying languidly stretched out and with a sudden flourish he put it on his head.

"Hey," cried Virgil, and Jasper could feel the dwarf scrabbling about on his head. "Hey, I'm stifling!" His voice was muffled.

"Oh," said Jasper, "I'll give you some fresh air right away. Wait a moment."

With the hat on his head he stepped out of the front door. "Wait a moment," he was muttering to himself, "I'll pay you out, you wretched dwarf!"

He walked up the road. There were the neighbours, still quarrelling with one another, especially with Mr Walker from opposite. Jasper behaved as if he were going somewhere, but as he was passing them, he politely took off his hat and said: "Good afternoon, everyone!"

They looked up. And went on looking. At Jasper, at his head, and the angry words stuck in their open mouths.

"A . . . dwarf . . .?"

They were not just saying it, they were seeing it. A tiny little man, sitting comfortably on Jasper's ruffled hair as he walked on, replacing the hat on his head. But, as they clearly saw, for a minute the dwarf waved to them with one arm and called: "Goodbye!"

They heard him clearly: Goodbye.

Jasper turned the corner, took the hat off again, lifted Virgil off his head and said: "That was your punishment."

"Charming," said Virgil. "Now take me home."

Jasper did so, but at home Cathy was crying because she had had bad marks at school. "For arithmetic," she sniffed. "Now I've got to learn all through the weekend. All the tables, by heart. The once-times table, the twice-times, the three-times – I don't want to do tables, I want to dance, I want to go to ballet."

"Oh dear," said her mother, "oh dear, poor Cathy."

But Jasper put Virgil on Cathy's shoulder to comfort her. And Virgil did comfort her. He whispered something in Cathy's ear . . .

13 Twice Times Tables

Poor Cathy. She had to spend the whole weekend learning multiplication tables. The once-times table was not all that difficult: once one is one, twice one is two, three ones are three – she could remember that. The twice-times table could be done, too, but the three-times table got more difficult and after that there were so many more – they could not be learned, could not be remembered.

But Virgil had an idea. He whispered something in her ear.

"What?" said Cathy. She had not understood.

Virgil whispered again and Cathy stopped sobbing and heard what he was saying: "Tonight you must sleep on one ear!"

"On one ear?"

"Yes," said Virgil. "Your right ear."

"And then?" she asked.

"You'll see," said Virgil, and he would say no more.

They went down to eat. "Ugh, sprouts!" cried Jasper, but father made him eat a few and then he got an extra spoonful from mother.

Virgil was sitting on the salt dish. But suddenly he lay down with one ear on the white cloth and said: "Hey, I can hear something. A mouse under the table."

The whole family shoved their chairs backwards, leaned forward and looked. "Where is it? I can't see anything! Pssst pssst!"

"I must have been wrong," said Virgil. He was panting a bit, as if he had run very fast across the table, and there was a green smudge on his jersey. And – Jasper could see – there was one sprout less on his plate and one more on his father's plate.

"Ahum," said mother.

"And as I was going to say," cried Virgil from the salt dish, "I am going to sleep in Cathy's left-hand ballet shoe tonight."

"Really?" said mother. "Does Cathy approve?"

Cathy nodded.

And that's how it was.

Virgil lay down comfortably but he did not go to sleep. In the middle of the night, when Cathy was lying cosily and peacefully asleep on one ear, Virgil climbed up the foot of the bed, crept over the blanket, crawled on to the pillow and began to whisper very softly in Cathy's other ear: "Once nine is nine, twice nine is eighteen, three nines are twenty-seven . . ." and so on, the whole of the nine-times table, the highest of all the tables under ten. And Virgil whispered it through nine times in a row, into

Cathy's ear while she slept. "Six nines are fifty-four, seven nines are sixty-three . . ." and Cathy slept and slept . . .

But next morning she said: "I had a dream, I had such a funny dream, I was dreaming that . . ."

She could not tell them anything more, she had forgotten the whole thing, but then Virgil said: "Do you know your three-times table?"

Cathy looked glum. "Once three is three," she began. "Twice three is seven, four threes are nine, five threes . . ."

"That doesn't sound too good," said Virgil. "What about nine times?"

"Ha ha!" cried Cathy. "I don't know that one at all. I've only got to learn that at the very end. I only know as far as once nine is nine," but suddenly she heard herself going on: "Twice nine is eighteen, three nines are twenty-seven, four nines are thirty-six, five nines are forty-five . . ." She rattled it off, the whole table, like an old-fashioned cash till, and then she gave a shout.

"My dream! That's what I dreamed, the nine-times table!"

"Yes," said Virgil, "and now you could say it in your sleep."

Cathy looked at him wide-eyed: "How did it happen, Virgil? How did it happen?"

"Oh well," Virgil murmured, "oh hum. Dwarfs' secret."

And so it went on: every night Virgil slept in the ballet slipper, one night in the left and the next night in the right, and every night Cathy slept on one ear, the first night on her right ear, the next night on her left, and while she was asleep Virgil crept on to her pillow and whispered a whole multiplication table in her ear: the eight times table eight times, the seven times table seven times, the six times, the five times, the four times, the three times, the twice . . .

Cathy could say them in her sleep.

On the next day that they had arithmetic, she repeated all of them. She made only one mistake: in the once times table. Virgil had not done that one because it is so easy.

But Cathy did not care. She wanted to go to her ballet class.

"Well," said father when he heard the tale. "So it's quite handy having a dwarf in the house after all. I'm glad I believe in them now."

"Right," said Virgil. "In that case I'm going to go off to have an evening stroll."

He jumped to the floor, went into the kitchen and scrambled out through the little cat door.

14 An Evening Stroll

Yes, Virgil scrambled out through the cat door to take an evening stroll; he did not even say goodbye to Cathy or to Jasper, because he was only going to take a quick walk and come back again directly.

Perhaps it would have been better if he had said goodbye, because the neighbours had a dog. Cinders, the one that Cathy had called dangerous, the one that bit, and was a brute.

Cinders saw and heard the cat door moving. She knew perfectly well that in former times a cat had always come through there. And Cinders did not like cats.

With an unexpectedly hard jerk she pulled the lead out of her master's hand and jumped through the hedge, where there was still a hole from all the earlier times that she had jumped through it.

"Come here!" shouted the neighbour.

It was no use. Cinders was storming towards the cat door to catch the cat, but she found Virgil.

"Well well, there's a wild one," thought the dwarf. He just had time to throw himself behind the rain barrel. "Bad dog!" he shouted.

Cinders' snap had missed and she went off her head. She barked at the top of her voice: "A cat, a cat, a cat!" as if she was trying to call in the whole neighbourhood, and she jumped to and fro in front of the rain barrel. But Virgil was climbing up behind it – it was close to the wall, so it was quite easy – and when Cinders stuck her nose under the barrel to sniff out the cat, Virgil was standing on top of it.

"What a bad dog," he muttered to himself. "We shall have to see about taming that. One, two, hop!" And the dwarf jumped from above onto the dog's neck. Well, that's what Virgil is like.

Cinders was not used to that kind of thing.

She jumped, turned her head in all directions, and shook herself, but Virgil hung on to her collar. Then Cinders began to run.

"Cinders! Come here!" shouted the neighbour.

But Cinders was flying up the street, trailing the loose lead behind her.

"Neighbour, what's going on?" cried mother. And father and Cathy and Jasper followed her out.

"What's the matter with your dog?"

"I don't know," said the neighbour. "I thought it was a cat but . . ."

"Virgil!" all four of them shouted at once. "He's caught Virgil!" And Cathy began to cry.

But that was not at all necessary. Virgil was riding comfortably on the dog's back and the dog was running and running. Right on to the moor.

There the dwarf leaned forward, put his face in the laid-back ear of the dog and began to whisper sweet words into it. "Oozy, moozy, snoozy . . ."

That is how you tame dogs.

Cinders slowed down and stopped, panting. She pricked up one ear and turned her head in order to hear the soft, sweet voice better.

"Silly," said the soft, sweet voice. "I'm not a cat, am I? I'm a dwarf. Can't you *smell* the difference?"

"Hum . . ." went the animal.

"What does a dog use his nose for otherwise?" said the voice.

"*His?*" cried the dog. "*His?* I'm a female, you know. You should say *her.*"

"Oh dear," cried Virgil. "Please don't be angry with me. I had forgotten." (After all, Cathy had told him that Cinders was a female.)

"Well, Miss Cinders," he said now. "You're a good dog. Now you can take me home again."

The dog turned round and began to walk back obediently across the moor. And the loose lead trailed after her.

"A little faster!" cried Virgil. "Up geegee, up!"

But then – of course – the loose lead caught on something. On the roots of a pine, and suddenly, whoops, Cinders was standing still.

Virgil had not thought of that. He tumbled over the dog's head and fell into the heather.

"Stupid!" shouted a cross voice. "Stupid! Watch where you're falling!"

Whose voice was that? . . .

15 Homecoming

"Stupid!" shouted the voice again, and this time Virgil recognised it.

It was the voice of Crooked Dirk, one of the other Nosegay Dwarfs, and he was shouting *stupid* because Virgil had fallen straight on to his barrow. A dwarf barrow, fully laden with pots of honey.

"Donkey!" shouted Crooked Dirk even louder, because everything had been overturned and the honey was dripping into the heather. "Our last supply. In any case, who goes falling off dogs!"

"Me," said Virgil. "Hallo, Crooked Dirk. How goes it with you?"

"Badly!" cried Crooked Dirk. "All our honey is spoiled. In any case, who goes riding on a dog?"

"Me," said Virgil again. "And it's very comfortable. I'll go and get you a new pot."

"Oh yes," said Crooked Dirk. "The bees will have enough left for sure, that's what *you* think."

"Oh no," said Virgil. "Jasper."

Crooked Dirk did not understand. "What is Jasper?" he asked.

"Jasper is not a what," said Virgil. "It's a boy."

"Oh," said Crooked Dirk. "That boy belonging to the human beings? The one who was here? Are you still living there?"

"Yes," said Virgil.

"And is that his dog?" asked Crooked Dirk, pointing to Cinders.

"No," said Virgil, "she belongs to the neighbour."

"I see," said Crooked Dirk. "Then you ought to be able to steer him better. Look at my barrow . . ."

But Virgil cried: "Him? Him? You ought to say her. It's a female. Her name is Cinders. Now say good-day to her politely."

"Oh," said Crooked Dirk. "Hallo, Miss Cinders." It sounded gruff, but he did make a little bow.

For answer the dog began to bark. She wanted to get away and go home. It was getting pretty dark by now.

Virgil climbed up along the lead to her collar and

sat down again on Cinders' back.

"Pull the lead off the root," he called down to Crooked Dirk. "Then I'll go and get you a pot of honey right away."

"This I have to see," muttered Crooked Dirk, unhooking the dog's lead.

Cinders ran on, on her way home. "Goodbye!" called Virgil.

Crooked Dirk looked after him, shaking his head. This bodes no good, he thought. When Virgil shouts goodbye it's usually for a long time . . .

Virgil was not thinking of anything. He leaned forward and whispered in the dog's ear: "Miss Cinders, just put me down at Jasper's back door." For he was thinking to himself: then I can crawl back in through the cat door and ask if Jasper can take a pot of honey to the moor on his bike. For Crooked Dirk.

It was a good plan all right, but when Cinders turned into the lane the neighbour was waiting for his dog and he was very angry.

"Here you! Disobedient beast!" he shouted. "You're very wicked!"

Cinders shrank down and shuffled slowly, head bowed, towards her master.

Away! thought Virgil to himself. I can walk that last bit to the cat door.

He climbed down round the collar to Cinders' throat and grasped the loose lead in order to slide down it to the ground. But at that very moment the neighbour seized hold of his disobedient dog by the collar. "Bad dog!" he shouted, and in his anger he tugged at the leather and dragged his dog in with him.

Cinders could scarcely breathe, her throat was so tightly pinched. She coughed with a strangled, choking sound. But Virgil could not get his breath either. The poor dwarf was caught fast between dog and collar and instead of slipping away unseen to Jasper's house he was dragged unseen into the neighbour's house. Once inside, he was locked up with the naughty dog as a punishment. Bang, the door shut.

Only then was the dwarf able to wriggle loose, get his breath and climb down to the floor. But once there, there he was, locked in.

There they both were.

Cinders by the door, whining softly.

The neighbour in his living-room in the comfortable chair, angrily rustling his newspaper.

And in the house next door Jasper and Cathy and their mother sat waiting anxiously for Virgil.

"That Cinders!" howled Jasper. "He's taken Virgil and ea . . . ea . . ."

"No, he hasn't," said mother. "Virgil is not caught that easily. I know for certain that he'll be back. He'll simply come back through the cat door."

"But *when?*" asked Cathy.

Mother did not know.

And father, when he came home, did not know either.

And there they sat. Until it was so late that they had to go to bed and sleep – all of them: the dog, the dwarf and the human beings.

But in the night something happened . . .

16 Whispering

Virgil had wrapped himself up in a rug for the night, in the neighbour's side room. He was sleeping like a baby. Cinders the dog had stopped whining and was sleeping too. Everyone was asleep. The lamps outside in the street were burning for nothing. There was no one about, not a person, not a dog, not a cat. Only the stars moved on, so slowly that you could not see that they were moving, but who ever looks anyway?

The curtains in the side room were still open of course and Sirius, which is the brightest star in the southern sky in winter, was shining into the room. His glittering eye shone straight into Virgil's face.

It woke the dwarf up.

Now where am I? he thought, half asleep. Inside or out? And who's that snoring? Is it Cathy? He unrolled himself from the rug and crept towards the snoring in a daze.

Is Cathy sleeping on the floor? he thought. Has

she fallen out of bed? Virgil put out his hand and jumped. "Hey, Cathy can't be that hairy? And she hasn't got such big ears, surely? And . . ."

"I sound like Red Riding Hood," thought Virgil.

And then, from fright, he found himself wide awake at last.

Oh, he thought, it's the dog.

But thinking of Cathy had given Virgil an idea. He crept close to the ear of the sleeping animal, and just as he had whispered to Cathy at night what she had to repeat the following day at school, so now he whispered into Cinders' ear what she had to do as soon as she woke up. In dog language, of course.

After that Virgil went back to sleep. The star Sirius crept behind the neighbour's chimney and an hour later light began to dawn.

Cinders woke up, yawned, stood up, stretched, yawned again, her mouth fearfully wide, and suddenly looked very alertly at the window.

As if there was something there.

Then the dog jumped on to the window sill, pushed off two flower pots of geraniums, which fell clatter-clatter to the floor, took the window knob in her teeth, clenched her jaws and began to worry it, growling. Just as if it were her prey.

Is that what Virgil had been whispering in her ear?

The dwarf, awakened by the row, climbed up the chair towards her. "No!" he shouted. "No, Miss Cinders, not like that!"

In dog language of course.

But Cinders was much too excited to listen. She

shook and pulled and pulled and shook at the window knob, and her tail wagged to and fro so wildly that two more flower pots with geraniums in them were swept off the window ledge.

"Turn it!" shouted Virgil. "You've got to turn it!"

For the window must be opened. That was what he had decided. That was what he had whispered to the dog in her sleep, but she was doing it wrong. The window stayed and Virgil could not get out.

And then the neighbour came into the room. In his pyjamas, because it was still so early. "What on earth!" he cried. "Cinders! Bad dog!" He too had been awakened by the noise and now he grabbed Cinders angrily by the collar and pulled her away.

"You naughty dog!" he cried. "I'm going to put you down in the cellar as a punishment."

Virgil had slipped quickly off the chair and dodged behind the radiator. "That's mean!" he shouted.

But in his anger the neighbour did not hear. Dragging Cinders away, he shut the door firmly behind him.

So I'm stuck again, thought the dwarf. I must get out of here. Jasper will be worried. And Cathy, and their mother and father . . . and the pot of honey, he went on in his thoughts. I've still got to take that pot of honey to the moor. I promised them yesterday. Virgil crept behind the door of the room.

The neighbour will be coming back any moment to clear up the flower pots, he thought. Then I shall slip out to Jasper, before he goes to school.

The little dwarf sat down to wait by the door.

17 A Tapping on the Window

Virgil waited and waited, but the door stayed shut. The neighbour had shut Cinders up in the cellar and had gone back to bed. Obviously the neighbour did not have to go to work that day.

But Jasper and Cathy did have to go to school. Virgil heard them squabbling.

"It's for me today."

"No, me."

"No, me."

"No, me!"

It was all about the red scarf, the beautiful red woollen scarf which they were allowed to wear in turn. But today it seemed to be both their turns. It also sounded as if they were both called ME.

"No, me" – "no, me" – "no, me!" Their voices re-echoed over the fence into the side room of the neighbour's house.

Virgil had jumped up, climbed up the chair on to the window ledge and was banging on the window.

But Jasper and Cathy went on shouting "no, me", "no, me", and noticed nothing.

Then Virgil picked up a fragment of one of the shattered flower pots and hammered on the glass with it as hard as he possibly could.

"Quiet!" Cathy cried then. "The neighbour's tapping on the window." They stopped and peered but could see nothing.

Then they heard the noise again.

Cathy and Jasper straightened up, had another good look and shouted in chorus: "Virgil!"

Their quarrel was forgotten. They scrambled through the gap in the hedge and ran to the window where they had seen their lost dwarf. They banged on the neighbour's front door and rang the bell.

Tingalingaling! They rang seven times, eight times. Cinders was barking herself mad in the cellar.

The neighbour had already jumped out of bed in a fury at all the row: banging on his window, shouts outside, barking inside, ringing at the doorbell . . .

He went first to the side room, but there was nothing to be seen there (he thought), and then to the front door. "Who's there?" he bellowed without opening the door.

"Us!" the children bellowed back again.

"Who's us? What do you want?"

"What did you say?"

"Our dwa-arf!" the children shouted at the closed door. "He's in your side room at the wi-indow!"

Then the neighbour grew really angry. He opened the letterbox in the front door and hissed at Cathy and Jasper: "If you go on once more about that dwarf and get me out of bed early in the morning for a pack of nonsense, I'll set the dog on you."

Cinders' barking from the cellar sounded terrible and dangerous.

Jasper and Cathy took a couple of steps backwards, turned round and rushed away, out of the gate and in through their own gate. Without saying a word they took their bicycles and rode off to school without the scarf. Mr Walker from opposite, who had naturally been staring at all the goings-on, stood gazing after them.

When they were at school Jasper said: "Don't cry, Cathy. Virgil will look after himself. At least we know he's alive now. And he's in good health, he banged so hard on the window pane!" Suddenly they both had to laugh.

The neighbour was not laughing. He did not feel like laughing at all. He took another look round his little room, because after all the dog had been behaving very strangely, pushing all the flower-pots off the window ledge and gnawing at the knob.

But a dwarf! Of course, that was rubbish, the neighbour thought. It was probably some animal or other . . .

He looked all round the room, but there was nothing there.

No, of course not. The neighbour had left the door into the passage open and as you will have realized, Virgil had slipped quickly through it.

But where was he to go? To the kitchen, to the living-room, or perhaps up the stairs?

18 A Bright Dog

The neighbour had gone back to bed to get some more sleep after all the disturbance. He turned over furiously so that the bed creaked as if it were about to break and he shut his eyes tightly. And slept.

He dreamed about a dwarf which pulled his nose hard and shouted: "Come and open the front door. I want to go out."

It was a ridiculous dream, but the neighbour slept and slept, he slept until late in the morning. And where was Virgil all this time? Virgil was in the kitchen, because he was hungry. But all the cupboards were too high: the breadboard and bin, the biscuits and everything were shut away high above his head. The butter, cheese and milk were in the refrigerator, where no dwarf could get at them. And Cinders was calling *whoof, whoof* from the cellar.

"Hey!" Virgil shouted. "Please Miss Cinders, stop barking for a minute."

"No!" shouted the dog (it sounded like *bownow!)*

"I want to get out *(owt)*."

"Yes," said Virgil, "but barking won't get the door open and I can't wake your master up, not even by pulling his nose." (The neighbour's dream had been true!)

"Wow!" cried Cinders. "I'll bite his nose."

"Oh yes," said Virgil, "but you'll have to get out of the cellar first." The dog was quiet now.

"And I'll tell you how to do it," said Virgil.

He began to explain, in the dwarfish way, how the dog could pull down the door handle with her paw.

"Ha, ha!" cried Cinders. "As if I didn't know that. But it doesn't work with this door."

"Oh," said Virgil, "in that case you have to push the latch with your nose."

"Rubbish!" cried Cinders.

"Pig-headed dog!" Virgil shouted back.

"Rude dwarf!" barked Cinders. "I'll eat you up!"

"Do that!" shouted Virgil. "But do come out."

That worked. Cinders pushed the door latch up with her nose and the door sprang open.

"There you are," said Virgil. "That's right, Miss Cinders. Now eat me up."

But if you say that to a dog, that's just what it doesn't do. Cinders didn't, either. "Where's my master?" she cried, running to and fro, from the kitchen to the living-room to the side room, but when she was about to go upstairs, Virgil cried:

"Stop!"

"Stop what?"

"Just stop," said Virgil. "Are you hungry?"

"Of course," said Cinders. "I'm always hungry."

"Then I'll give you something to eat."

"WHAT?" Cinders came downstairs again, really curious now. "Something to eat? From a little person like you? How?"

Virgil said: "Put your ear down here."

And the dwarf whispered in the special dog language exactly what Cinders had to do, and how.

When the neighbour woke up an hour later and came downstairs into the kitchen he stood stock-still.

There was his dog, sitting on a chair at the table with a plate in front of her, from which she had just licked the last bits of mincemeat. Mincemeat from the refrigerator! How . . .

The neighbour's jaw dropped slowly. But there were so many things he wanted to say at once that the words stuck in his throat. And as he stared with open mouth, Cinders picked up the well-licked plate in her teeth and carried it to the sink. Then she pushed the cupboard open with her nose, worked a new, unopened pot of honey out with her paw, let it roll across the floor and pushed it with her nose, rolling it down the passage to the front door. A pot of honey!

The neighbour was too flabbergasted to see that under Cinders' neck, inside her collar, there was something that was not usually there: a little dwarf. A little dwarf who was whispering all the time to the dog, telling her exactly what to do. A little dwarf who had promised to take a pot of honey to his friend on the moor.

Cinders gave a low whine at the front door, which in human language means: "Let me out."

19 Honey to the Moor

The neighbour was bewildered. My dog, he thought, all-a-quiver. My dog has suddenly become intelligent – she has human intelligence. H – how – what . . .

"Can you talk as well?" he asked the animal suddenly. "Do you understand me? I mean . . ."

But of course Cinders did not understand because the neighbour, her master, could not ask her in dog language. Only Virgil, hidden under her collar, understood. But he did not answer. And when the neighbour went on standing there without opening the front door the dwarf whispered into the dog's ear:

"Whine as if you've got to go out. It will work."

So Cinders barked in a different tone and it certainly did work; every master understands that language from his dog.

"Oh Cinders, I will let you out at once," her master cried. "Wait a minute." He took the lead and was about to fasten it to Cinders' collar.

"No!" whispered Virgil. "Not on the lead. Growl angrily!"

"Grrr!" went Cinders.

Her master jumped backwards. "Nice doggy," he said soothingly. "Sweet dog. You *are* a good dog."

Her master did not think she was good at all, but he had become a little frightened of his own dog. She was behaving so strangely. Now she was even beginning to scratch at the door, she clearly needed to get out in a hurry.

"Off you go then," said her master. "Off you go. But not into the road. And don't run away!"

He stepped warily past the dog, turned the front door knob and pulled it open. Cinders picked up the honey pot in her teeth. They did not grip on the smooth glass, but she was able to hold on to the lid with difficulty, and out she went with the pot.

"Now I know," muttered the neighbour. "I'm still dreaming!" And he gave himself a terribly hard pinch on the arm. But he was not asleep, he was wide awake and what he saw was really happening. Cinders walked up the garden path, out of the gate, up the road to the right, without sniffing round anywhere, without crouching to do her business, without looking round, and with the honey pot between her teeth.

"Like a – like a human being," the neighbour murmured. "A human being, going to deliver a parcel somewhere."

"Cinders!" he called. "Cinders, *here!*"

He might just as well have shouted at his dustbin.

The dog did not even look round.

Well I never! thought the neighbour. He was finding the whole thing rather creepy, and there was Mr Walker from opposite, staring away with a false grin on his face. Mr Walker was enjoying himself – he liked to see a disobedient dog that did not come when her master called. Ha ha!

The neighbour shut the front door, completely baffled.

But Virgil went on swinging comfortably on the dog collar, like a sailor in his hammock, singing a cheerful ditty:

> "Come on dog, you're all right!
> Hold that honey pot good and tight,
> And carry me quite safe and sure
> To my dwarf friends on the . . ."

"Hey! Turn left here!"

Some people did give the dog an odd look: a big beast like that, walking along with a pot in its mouth without looking round, and apparently singing . . . But nobody dared to stop her.

> "And carry me quite safe and sure
> To my dwarf friends on the moor!"

That was where they were going – to the moor. To the molehill under which the Nosegay Dwarfs lived in wintertime.

"Put the pot down here," said Virgil when they reached it.

Cinders wanted to start digging in the molehill at once, but Virgil said: "Stop, are you mad, that's the front door of our house, keep off!" And putting his hands to his mouth he called: "Dirk! Crooked Dirk! Hallo!"

After a short time Crooked Dirk's head appeared. "You've been a long time," he said. "We were waiting and waiting. Where's the honey?"

Virgil pointed to the pot.

"Hm," said Crooked Dirk. "That's not bad. Thank you. Are you coming in?"

"Not me," said Virgil. "I'm all right where I am, with Jasper. Goodbye!"

And he let Cinders carry him home to Jasper with whom he intended to spend the whole of the winter. Much warmer and roomier than in that cramped molehill.

But halfway home Cinders suddenly stopped and stuck her nose in the air. She could smell something.

20 Freedom!

Cinders could smell something. Cinders was sniffing something. Dogs have noses which are really terrific. They can smell a sick ant half a mile off.

But Cinders could smell something else, and she was running towards it.

"Hey, hey!" cried Virgil. "Where are you off to?" The dwarf peered out from under the dog's collar. "You're supposed to be going home!"

But Cinders was not listening. When a dog gets the scent of something in its nose, something that excites it, you cannot hold it back with words – not even if you speak dog language as Virgil did.

So Cinders ran on, further and further, towards the edge of the moor.

And at the edge of the moor lived Aunt Cuckoo. Aunt Cuckoo lived there alone in a large house. She too was large, with a large nose and large black spectacles and a couple of black hairs on her chin. She snipped them off once a year, at Christmas time, because that was when she went to church. Aunt Cuckoo was an extraordinary person. In the war, when her bicycle had been taken by the soldiers, she used to go to the baker's shop on a scooter, pushing herself along. And because there were no street lamps at that time, when she had to go out in the evening she wore a white sheet and rang a bell so that she would not be run over. She was like a kind of ghost on the road. Aunt Cuckoo! And now she had a dog.

The dog was the most pathetic creature in the world. He did not even have a name. "Hush," Aunt Cuckoo would say to him. "Dog, hold your hush." That was the only thing she ever said to him, all day long, whenever he barked, because the dog was a watchdog. He sat outside in a cage, night and day, in order to bark when there was trouble afoot. But he did not know the difference between trouble and the postman, or the plumber, or the gasman, or the dustman or Aunt Cuckoo's nice nieces and nephews who came to visit her at Christmas time, so he barked and barked at everyone who came up the garden path. And every time Aunt Cuckoo shouted: "Hold your hush, hold your hush, hold your hush." In the end the dog thought his name was Hush. Not a bad thing.

And oh, how Hush longed to be allowed to run free just once. Just once. But Aunt Cuckoo never let him out, because she was afraid that at that very moment a thief would come.

And it was Hush the dog and his great longing that Cinders had just smelled. Dogs have a nose for that. Cinders ran into Aunt Cuckoo's garden, went over to the cage and stopped in front of the wire.

"Hallo, hallo! Come and play with me on the moor," she said, her tail wagging.

Hush began to wag too, but that meant: "How can I possibly? I'm shut in, aren't I? Can't you see, you donkey? I can't get out. Not ever. However much I would like to."

"Is that all?" Cinders wagged back. "Wait a minute. I shall open the cage for you." And she said to Virgil: "Can you explain how to do it?"

But then Hush began to bark ferociously, with rage. "Are you making fun of me? Making fun? Making fun? I've sat shut up here for years and then you come along, a free dog, to tease me and to go on as if . . ."

Then he stopped barking. Not because Aunt

Cuckoo was shouting HUSH! – Aunt Cuckoo was not at home – but because Hush had noticed a little dwarf under Cinders' collar, whispering something in Cinders' ear, after which the dog began to worry the catch of the wire door with her jaws, nibbling and wiggling, until the door swung open with a rusty squeak.

"Wuuuff!" went Hush, leaping out. At that moment a shrill voice shouted: "Hush!"

It was Aunt Cuckoo, who had just come home. She almost fell off her bike with astonishment at what she saw.

But Hush was no longer prepared to hold his hush. He was racing, rushing, flying on to the moor, with Cinders behind him.

"Stop!" shouted Virgil. "Not so fast! I'm being shaken to bits!"

But Cinders too had completely lost her head. The two dogs raced round and round, jumped, barked, bowled each other over and played all the tricks they knew at once. They were very naughty dogs.

Poor Virgil. No sailor in the worst of storms has ever been shaken up as badly as the poor little Nosegay Dwarf under Cinders' collar.

And that was only the beginning of the dogs' play.

21 Dogs at Play

"Stop it, stop it, stop it!" shouted Virgil, who was really cross with Cinders by now. But the dog went on racing round, jumping over the heather, together with her friend Hush. "Stand still, I tell you!"

It was no good, until the two dogs grew tired and sat down – Cinders and Hush: two bouncing beasts, sitting opposite each other, panting, long red tongues hanging from wide open mouths.

"I say," said Hush, "how did you get hold of that?"

"What?" asked Cinders.

"That dwarf under your collar."

"Oh," said Cinders. "I got it from the neighbours."

"From the neighbours!" said Hush.

He sniffed at Virgil, but Virgil cried: "Leave off! Take your wet nose away, ugh! And now take me home, Cinders."

"Well, well," said Hush. "The dwarf can talk."

But Cinders said: "He can *think*. And that's why I'm free."

Then a furious voice rang across the moor: "Dog! Come *here!*"

It was Aunt Cuckoo in her long coat, starting across the moor to get her watchdog back.

Hush jumped to his feet, but not from obedience; he did not want to go back to his cage at all. "Come on," he shouted to Cinders, and then the two began to run again. They ran in circles round the furious Aunt Cuckoo, and they became extraordinarily rowdy. Here and there other people had appeared on the moor, people who were simply taking an evening stroll and letting their dogs out.

And Cinders and Hush made for these dogs and began to stir them up. "Come with us," they shouted, "come with us. Never mind about your master. We're all going to have a bit of a lark!"

There was such a barking and running and shouting and whistling. Six, seven, eleven, twelve dogs and puppies were frolicking together, some with loose ends of lead behind them, others free, but all of them equally extremely bad and wicked and disobedient. And their masters and mistresses in their respectable hats and respectable off-duty coats stood there shouting, Ricky, Micky, Dicky, and Hector, Senator, Blackie, Jumbo, Rover, Cleo, or whatever the dogs' names were, "Come here, *here,* to your master, to your mistress, oh, you bad, bad dog!"

All the sounds came out together, all mixed up. If the dogs had wanted to obey they would not have been able to, the language the humans spoke was impossible to understand.

And Virgil? Virgil was no longer playing any part in events at all.

But at long last even those twelve dogs were tired and breathless from their running and racing. One after another they went back to their master or mistress, where they were put on the lead and spoken to severely. Even Hush crept over to Aunt Cuckoo. And it must be said that since that day Aunt Cuckoo was a little bit nicer to her watchdog. He was allowed out for some time every afternoon and on Sundays he came and sat on a cushion in the living-room. All thanks to Virgil!

Cinders too went home, slowly. Cinders was afraid of her master; he was going to be terribly cross – cross, cross, cross, because she had run away for the second time.

Head bowed, she went in through the garden gate and scratched at the front door.

But it was all right.

"Drat the dog!" cried the neighbour when he opened the front door. "Drat the dog, where have you been?"

And that was all he said. He was still afraid of Cinders, afraid that she was going to do some more strange things. So he did not dare to be angry.

"All right then, go to your basket," he said.

Cinders did so, good as gold.

And then the neighbour noticed.

"Drat the dog," he cried, "where is your collar?"

Cinders' neck was bare. The collar had gone. And so, of course, had Virgil.

22 An Idea

When Jasper came out of school that afternoon with Cathy, he went at once to his mother and asked if Virgil had come back yet.

"No," said his mother, "I haven't seen him."

"Oh dear," cried Jasper, "then he must still be at the neighbour's house."

"The neighbour's?" asked mother.

"Yes," cried Cathy, "we saw him there this morning. Behind the window."

"Virgil?" asked mother. "How could you have?'

"We did, we did!" The children told her that they had seen Virgil at the window in the neighbour's side room and they told her how cross the neighbour had been when they had rung his bell early in the morning.

"Well," said their mother, 'I'll go over with you then."

They rang the neighbour's bell. Cinders barked. The neighbour opened the door.

"Good afternoon," said mother. "Can we have our dwarf back?"

Jasper and Cathy thought that the neighbour was going to be terribly angry, but instead of being angry the neighbour said: "My dog, my dog," in a very strange voice.

"No," said mother. "Dwarf. Our dwarf."

The neighbour looked at her as if she was speaking Chinese and said: "My dog is behaving so strangely! Eating from a plate on the table, and running away with a pot of honey in her mouth and coming back without a collar."

"Well I never," said Mother.

But Jasper and Cathy were shouting "Virgil!" very loudly inside. "Virgil, are you there?"

Cinders began to bark even louder, but Virgil did not appear.

"I'm so afraid that she's going mad," the neighbour went on. "She was away all morning. Running round. On the moor I think, because her fur . . ."

"On the moor?" cried Jasper.

"Yes," said the neighbour. "And the last time too, when . . ."

But Jasper had run off. He jumped over the hedge, picked up his bike and rode very fast down the street.

"Jasper!" called his mother and Cathy. "Where are you going?"

But they might as well have been asking in Chinese too, because they got no answer.

When the neighbour had talked about the moor

Jasper had had an idea – a crazy idea, in fact. Jasper suddenly knew for certain that Virgil was on the moor. Taken there by Cinders the dog, in one way or another. Back to his little dwarf friends, of course.

Jasper steered straight for the place, which he now knew: along the gravel path, then left, right at the fourth pine tree, then straight on for a bit, put the bike down, walk on to the little birch tree, past the hollow and behind that must be the molehill, the molehill, the mole . . .

But Jasper saw no sign of a molehill. The hollow was not the right hollow, the little birch tree was really a rowan tree, no, this was not the place where the Dwarfs of Nosegay lived.

Jasper looked about him and began to walk round in a steadily widening circle, with his eyes on the ground, because he must and would find that molehill.

"Virgil!" he shouted. "Virgil!"

Of course there was no answer.

But his foot caught on something. At first he thought it was a tough root of heather, but it was something else. It was a leather collar: Cinders' collar.

And beside it: beside it lay Virgil!

Virgil, with closed eyes, motionless, deathly pale.

Jasper stood as if turned to stone. Then he knelt down, stooped over the little dwarf, touched his cheek very very gently with one finger and whispered: "Vir–Virgil? Are – are you still alive?"

There was no answer, no movement, not even the flicker of an eyelid.

Uhhh, thought Jasper.

He picked the dwarf up very carefully, put him under his jacket, went back to his bicycle, rode home steering with one hand, walked into the kitchen and began to cry. "Mum, Mummy!" He put Virgil on the table. Still pale as death and unmoving.

Jasper's mother looked, stooped, put her ear to Virgil's chest, straightened again and said: "He's still alive, even if he's not kicking".

Then she carried Virgil very gently upstairs and put him in Cathy's ballet shoe, warmly covered with a little blanket, and told Jasper:

"We shall have to get a doctor for him. Just to be sure. But who?"

Well, yes, who?

There were animal doctors, of course, but dwarf doctors? Who would you call to see a sick dwarf?

23 The Doctor

There lay Virgil, pale and motionless under a little blanket in Cathy's ballet shoe. Very sick.

"But where did you find him?" Cathy asked Jasper.

"Somewhere," said Jasper. "Somewhere on the moor. He was lying there. Beside Cinders' collar."

"Did Cinders bite him?" asked Cathy, half weeping.

"No, no," said mother. "There's no wound on Virgil. Nowhere on his whole body."

"But what's the matter with him then?"

Yes, what was the matter with Virgil? The doctor would have to tell them. But Mother had still been unable to think which doctor she could ask to come and look at him.

"The animal doctor," said Jasper.

"No, our doctor," said Cathy.

Then father came home. Father was an old-fashioned father who knew everything. He said:

"Oh, we'll get Doctor Hedges for that. He knows about gnomes. I'll ring him up at once."

Father telephoned.

And not long afterwards he was telling them: "Yes, the doctor is coming. But he lives a long way off so it will be some time before he gets here."

But they had scarcely begun to wait when a car stopped in front of the door, one of those cars which goes very fast, and at once a little doctor came popping out. Doctor Hedges. Quickly, quickly he picked up his brown bag; quickly, quickly he walked to the front door, took out a big key (a key which fits all doors), stepped inside without ringing, crick-crack into the hall. He shouted: "Hedges here! Patient upstairs I expect?" and ran up the stairs.

Well, well, well. When father and mother and Cathy and Jasper came up too, the doctor was already standing over Virgil with his glasses on his nose and two tubes in his ears.

"Quite," he said. "I've seen it already. Just as I thought: *somnolentio per trauma capitis*. I'll give you a prescription for the chemist."

With one hand the doctor wrote something on a slip of paper, with the other he returned his stethoscope to the bag, and with a third hand (so it seemed) he buttoned up his coat. And when his legs were already moving he said: "Keep nice and warm, lots of rest, lots to drink, I'll come back next week," and he was gone.

Well, well, well.

"A lightning visit," said father.

"I feel quite dazed," said mother.

"He . . . he wasn't surprised at all," said Cathy, "he wasn't surprised that Virgil was a dwarf."

"No," said father, "of course not."

"But what *has* Virgil got?" asked Jasper.

None of them knew the answer to that, until someone else said something. He said: "I haven't got anything at all."

All four of them turned round. There sat Virgil, in the ballet shoe, wide awake and as fit as a fiddle.

"Virgil, you're ill!" they all cried together. "You have to keep warm and quiet and drink a lot and . . ."

"Ill?" said Virgil. "How did you get that idea?"

"But you . . . you were lying so *still,*" cried Jasper, "and the doctor . . ."

"Doctor?" said Virgil. "Was that a doctor?"

"Yes," said father. "And he's made you better very quickly, I must say."

Suddenly they were all very merry and Jasper cried: "Virgil, what did happen? How did you land up on the moor?"

"Moor?" said Virgil. "Oh yes, of course, now I remember."

And he told them everything that had happened with Cinders and the neighbour and the pot of honey and Aunt Cuckoo's dog and all the other dogs who had had fun and games on the moor. "And then, I was so dreadfully shaken up under Cinders' collar," the dwarf told them, "that I undid the buckle. Then I fell on the ground with the thing and – well, after that I don't really know. I expect I must have fallen on my head and my thoughts got a bit mixed up. But I can think again now. At least . . ." He looked at the four of them. "Am I thinking all right?" he asked.

"You are," mother told him.

Virgil shook his head hard. "And now?" he asked.

Cathy began to laugh. "We can't see what you're thinking, can we?" she said.

"Oh yes," said Virgil, "oh yes, because I'm thinking: then how did I get back here from the moor?"

Then father said: "Now you are thinking well, Virgil. It was Jasper. He went and looked for you and found you on the moor. And brought you home."

"Jasper," said Virgil. He said no more. But he looked at Jasper for a minute and then he looked away and he wiped his sleeve across his eyes.

Were those dwarf tears?

24 Under Arrest

Virgil was completely better. Dwarfs recover so quickly; the doctor did not even have to come back once.

"Thank you very much, Jasper," said Virgil next morning. "Thank you very much for rescuing me."

"It was nothing," said Jasper.

"And can I go on living here this winter?" asked the dwarf.

"Of course you can," was the answer.

They were sitting at breakfast: Jasper, Cathy and their mother, but father was upstairs shaving himself, he was late that morning.

"Go and give your father a call, Cathy," said mother. "Tell him it's a quarter past eight."

"But it's only ten past," said Cathy.

"That's why," said mother. "Then he'll still be in time."

Cathy went to the bottom of the stairs. "Dad!" she began to call, but then the front door bell rang.

"Dad! It's ten – I mean a quarter past eight!" and at the same time she opened the front door to let in her friend Judy who came to pick her up for school in the morning.

"What?" father called down.

"It's a quarter past ten! – I mean ten past a quarter!" shouted Cathy. "Hello Ju . . ."

But it was not Judy at all. On the step stood a policeman, as large as life.

"Young lady," he said, "young lady, may I be permitted to enter?"

"Wh-what on earth?" stammered Cathy. She ran back to the living-room. "Mum, a policeman!"

Mother put down her teacup. "Just give Dad a shout," she said.

Cathy ran back to the stairs. "Daddy! A policeman!"

"What?" called father. "What's that you're shouting?"

"A po-lice-man!" shouted Cathy. "Come down now! He's at the door!"

Father came downstairs, his cheeks snowy-white from the shaving soap. "Are you having a game with me?" he asked.

"No, no," said Cathy nervously. "Here he is. Here is my father, Mr Policeman," she said to the policeman.

"Well sir," the policeman began, "complaints have been reaching the station."

"Well?" said father. "Come in for a moment. And let's hear all about it."

The policeman wiped his feet, stamping them on

the mat, hung his cap up on the coat-rack and followed father indoors.

"Hallo!" said mother. "Good morning, Officer! We had you here once before, didn't we?"

"That's right, madam."

"Oh yes, now I see," said father. "You brought our Jasper back in the middle of the night. Is it about him again?"

"No sir," said the policeman. "It's about a – a resident of yours."

"Oh dear," murmured mother. And Jasper reached for the sugar bowl on which Virgil was sitting, to pick up the dwarf and hide him away somewhere. But Virgil jumped on top of the tea cosy and shouted in a clear voice:

"It's about me, isn't it, policeman? A complaint from our neighbour, I expect?"

The policeman looked at the tea cosy, took his pocket-book out again, turned the pages, read a few

lines, looked at the tea cosy again and nodded.

"The description fits," he said. "Unusually small, 'dwarf' in quotation marks. Can I have your name?"

"My name is Virgil," said Virgil.

The policeman wrote Virgil in his little book.

"And after that? Surname?"

"Nosegay," said Virgil.

The policeman wrote Nose Gay in his little book.

"With a hyphen?" he asked.

"No, no," said Virgil. "No hyphen. All one word."

The policeman wrote *no hyphen, all one word* in his little book. He wrote everything down in his little book and Jasper's lower lip was beginning to tremble. What was going to happen to Virgil? Would he have to go with the policeman?

"Officer," asked father, still with his snowy cheeks, "what does all this mean? What are the complaints?"

"I am not authorized to inform you as to that, sir," said the policeman. "I am instructed to arrest and accompany the accused to the police station for further questioning."

There it was. Jasper shouted, "NO" very loudly. But Virgil cried: "Oh, that will be fun!"

25 At the Police Station

"I think it's fun," said Virgil again, when the policeman stood up to take him down to the police station. But Jasper and Cathy and father and mother did not think it was fun at all.

"But he hasn't done anything!" cried Jasper.

"Virgil never does anything!" cried Cathy.

"What could a little dwarf like that do?" asked mother.

And father asked: "Who has made the complaints, then?"

"Well," said the policeman, "the complaints came from the whole neighbourhood and they were brought to us by a Mr Walker."

Jasper turned red with anger. "That mean old deaf-ears!" he shouted.

Then Virgil, speaking from the tea cosy on which he was still standing, said: "Why are all of you going on grumbling and yackety-yacking? I don't mind going along with the policeman. I very much want to see a police station from the inside."

"Yes, but Virgil," Jasper began.

But the dwarf said: "It's only for a short time, Jasper. As soon as it gets boring I'll say goodbye to the police and come back again."

It was perhaps not very sensible of Virgil to say that aloud when the policeman was there, but it made Jasper laugh like anything.

"Haven't you got a cap?" Virgil asked the policeman. "I'll only go with you underneath your cap."

The policeman went to fetch it from the coat rack and held it out for the dwarf, so that he could step inside.

"No," said Virgil. "I want to go on your head, under the cap. Lean down!"

The policeman bent towards the tea cosy, as if he were making a deep bow before the little dwarf, and Virgil ruffled his hair first to make sure it was clean.

"A respectable policeman's head," he announced, and climbed onto the curls.

"Stand up! Right! And now: cap on! Right!"

The policeman saluted the family and the smothered voice of Virgil called: "Goodbye!"

And so the dwarf was taken to the police station. And deaf old Mr Walker opposite, and the neighbour with Cinders the dog, and the other neighbours and next-to-neighbours were all standing staring behind their lace curtains. It made them miss the bus and get to work late, except for Mrs Stonehouse-Dashwood; she was not staring, she was sitting at her piano and studying difficult scales with a lot of black dots.

At the police station the sergeant was already waiting for the policeman.

"Well, Fisher? No arrest?"

"Oh yes, sergeant," said the policeman.

"I can't see much sign of it," said the sergeant.

The policeman took off his cap and set Virgil down on the table, small, immovable, stiff as a post and stock-still. Like a statuette.

The sergeant looked and looked and then he started to speak to the policeman in a dangerous, hissing voice: "Listen, er, Fisher, you're not in the police force for these kind of tricks, eh? You can go and work at the fairground with little tricks like that. *Get it?!*"

PC Fisher turned fiery red. He said: "But sergeant, this is the dwarf, the very same one I reported on last time."

The sergeant stared at the policeman for a long time, sighed deeply and said: "Fisher, do you want

me to send you to a psychiatrist?"

"N-no, sergeant," stammered the policeman. And to Virgil he said: "Come on, say something," and he gave the dwarf a nudge in the back.

"Stop that!" cried Virgil angrily. He stumbled over the blotter and fell with his nose in the sergeant's ashtray.

"Atishoo! Pooh, what a mess!" he cried.

The sergeant had shot backwards on his chair and was staring open-mouthed.

"What a smelly cigar you smoke, don't you!" shouted the little dwarf. He brushed the ash from his clothes, making a lot of dirty smudges on the neat letter the sergeant was busy writing.

PC Fisher cleared his throat politely and asked: "Do I still have to go to to the skytryatwist?"

Then the sergeant exploded. "NO!" he bellowed. And: "What's that dwarf doing on my table! Take him away! To the cells with him!"

But Virgil said: 'Oh no, I don't want to go there. I want to see the police station, not the cells."

"Talking too now?" cried the sergeant.

"Yes," said Virgil. "Quite a bit. And I'm little too. Nice and little, so I can slip away through the bars if you put me in the cell."

Then the sergeant, still in that dangerous hissing tone, said: "Fisher, haven't we got one of those old bird-cages in the Lost Property? Go and fetch one, quick as a flash."

At the same time he grasped Virgil by the collar and held him tightly.

"Quick as a flash, Fisher!" cried the sergeant.

26 Interrogation

PC Fisher returned like lightning, with a rusty old bird cage from the Lost Property Department, and the sergeant shut Virgil inside it with his own hands.

The cage was set on top of the table, right under the sergeant's nose.

"Good," he said. "That's better. Now we can interrogate the prisoner. Your name?"

Virgil had climbed up and was sitting on the perch in the bird's cage. He said: "Peep!"

"Peep," said the sergeant. "Quite." And to the constable he said: "Write it down, Fisher: Peep."

"Yes, but Sergeant," the constable began, "his name is . . ."

"Silence!" cried the sergeant. "All you have to do is write." And turning back to the cage, he said: "First name?"

Virgil had jumped down from the perch and was rummaging in the empty food bowl. "Peep, peep!" he went.

Slowly the sergeant's face turned red. "Are you making fun of me?" the face thundered.

Virgil hopped back to the other side of the cage and rummaged in the drinking bowl. "Peep, peep, peep!" he cried.

A smothered *hic* came from the constable's throat. And then another.

The sergeant shot to his feet. "Are you standing there laughing, Fisher?" he shrieked.

"Oh no, Sergeant, not at all," said the constable in a stifled voice. "But I think the dwarf has changed into a canary."

"Huh?" went the sergeant. He stared with narrowed eyes at PC Fisher. Would he have to go to the psychiatrist after all, or what was wrong with him?

Meanwhile Virgil had opened the little door of the rusty cage. And out he stepped.

"Hah!" he said. "I wasn't a canary bird at all! I was a tropical Bird of Paradise. Couldn't you see that?"

The sergeant made a grab and caught the dwarf.

"You ought to know by now," cried Virgil. "If you put me back in the cage, I shall only be able to say 'peep.' And in any case, I'm not going to run away. I shall only do that if it gets really boring here."

PC Fisher started to *hic* again, but the sergeant said: "Out with you, then," and went on with his interrogation.

Virgil was now sitting on the edge of the ashtray and again he gave his name, with all his first names, family names, street names, names of place of birth (all on the moor, on the moor, on the moor), and

Fisher sat scratching and scratching and scratching away until his ball-point nearly ran out.

"Quite," said the sergeant. "So you're a dwarf which does not exist, but which is sitting in front of me now. Hum! You have set the whole neighbourhood by the ears, committed a nuisance by noise, spread terror, loosed dogs and incited them to riot, forced an entrance into your neighbour's house, and stolen a pot of honey and a dog collar."

"Yes," said Virgil. "That's right. The collar is still on the moor. And I gave the pot of honey to my friends. But Jasper will pay for it, you know."

"I see," said the sergeant. "But all this nuisance you have caused, that can't go on. You'll have to leave the neighbourhood."

"Not at all," said Virgil. "I shouldn't dream of it. I'm staying there until the winter is over."

"Are you asking to be put back in the cage?" asked the sergeant threateningly.

"Yes, I am," said Virgil. "I can get out of it again anyway. You are behaving just as idiotically as the neighbours, sergeant. *They* make the nuisance, not *me*. It's *always* human beings, who *always* blame other people."

The sergeant struck his fist on the table so hard that the ashtray with Virgil on it jumped in the air.

"You need not write that last bit down, Fisher!" he thundered.

Virgil had run straight to the edge of the table.

"Now I can feel that it's getting really boring here," he said. "I've seen all I want to. Goodbye!"

And he jumped into the wastepaper basket.

27 In Flight

Virgil made a soft landing in the wastepaper basket. It was full of crumpled paper: all kinds of old summonses and parking tickets and also the greasy paper in which the sergeant had had his sandwiches wrapped.

"Bah," thought Virgil, "what mucky paper! I must get out of here quickly."

But the wastepaper basket was really a metal box and it's not so easy to get out of those. And in addition the sergeant quickly placed a large, heavy book on top of it like a lid, so that not even a flea would have been able to creep out.

"Got you!" he told PC Fisher.

"Yes sir," said Fisher. "But what now?"

The sergeant scratched his head. "Humph." Virgil in the wastepaper basket was not quite the same thing as Virgil in the hand.

"Hey!" shouted the dwarf, his voice a muffled echo. "Hey, I'm going to pass out from this smell."

You stay there, thought the sergeant, but at that moment the door opened and the inspector came in.

"Morning, George," he said to the sergeant. "Have you got the atlas in here? Can I have it for a moment?"

"Atlas?" said the sergeant. "Atlas? NO!"

"What do you mean 'No'? What's this? I want to look at the atlas this minute!" cried the inspector.

"You can't!" said the sergeant.

The atlas was the big, heavy book on top of the wastepaper basket. Suddenly the inspector saw it lying there. "You're not going to throw it away, are you?" he cried. "Surely you're not going to throw an expensive atlas in the wastepaper basket?"

"No, er no, no. It's a sort of lid," the sergeant explained.

"Lid? Ah! Have you caught a mouse?"

"Well, no, not a mouse. A, er . . ."

"A prisoner," said PC Fisher.

"A . . . ha, ha, good joke," said the inspector.

But PC Fisher did not smile. He said: "A dwarf, so to speak, sir. A real one too. With a record!"

The inspector looked from one to the other, but before he had said anything else the muffled echo came from the wastepaper basket: "I've got bloater paste all over me! Please take that book away!"

The inspector half-closed his eyes. "What was that?" he asked.

"That, sir," PC Fisher replied helpfully – and he began to read from his little book – "that is Nosegay, first name: Virgil, street name : On the Moor, place name: On the Moor, date of birth . . ."

The inspector interrupted him. "Yes yes, that's enough of your little jokes," and without an apology he took the atlas away, picked up the wastepaper basket, turned it upside down and shook it empty.

All the old crumpled summonses and parking tickets, the greasy sandwich paper and Virgil rolled across the rug.

"Hey, hey," cried the dwarf, "I think your bloater paste was off, sergeant."

All three of them stood there speechless, but Virgil did not wait to be caught again. He vanished through the door which the inspector had left open, with his familiar, "Goodbye"!

But that did not mean he was outside. Not by any means. First of all he had to go through the secretary's room, past Miss Niven, then along the passage, then past the counter where Constables Stoker, German and Hill were sitting, then through the swing door, across the lobby, through a revolving door and down the steps, before he could reach the street at last. A long journey for a dwarf.

On the way there Virgil had made the trip comfortably under PC Fisher's cap. But now, on the way back, he was quite alone, in flight, pursued by the sergeant, the inspector and PC Fisher.

"Stop him!" they shouted.

The secretary, Miss Niven, stopped typing and asked: "Who?"

"The prisoner!" cried the sergeant.

"I can't see anything," she said. "I can't see anyone. And no one has been through here, either."

28 The Typewriter

What had become of Virgil? He had slipped through the door which the inspector had left open when he came in. But then where had he gone?

The secretary, Miss Niven, said: "I simply haven't seen anything, sir."

"But he must have come through here!" said the inspector sharply.

And the sergeant cried: "A prisoner for questioning!"

"Good gracious," said Miss Niven. "Was he dangerous? He's not behind the curtain, is he?"

The sergeant looked behind the curtain, a coarse grey police station curtain, which really should have gone to the dry cleaner's.

"No," he said. "And he's not dangerous either. You'd better send that curtain to the dry cleaner's."

But when he turned round he tripped over the bottom drawer of the desk. Miss Niven always left that drawer open.

"Ouch! Now, Miss Niven, how often have I told you that you must keep that drawer shut!"

"Oh, good gracious, I had forgotten all about it again, sir!" cried Miss Niven. "I'm so sorry." She pushed the drawer shut with a bang.

The inspector had already gone off with PC Fisher in search of Virgil and the sergeant limped behind them.

Miss Niven went on typing, tickety-tickety-tick, one letter after another, and she opened the drawer again to get out an envelope. There were at least a hundred envelopes in the drawer and Miss Niven had to take out one for each letter, which was why she always left the drawer open. She did not even need to look down, and that was how it happened that this time she pulled out, not an envelope, but a dwarf. It happened so quickly that she had almost rolled him into the typewriter.

"Hee, hee," laughed Virgil. "You seem very nervous!"

Miss Niven gave a shriek and dropped the dwarf. "Who, what, how . . ." she began.

"I am Virgil Nosegay," said the dwarf. "The sergeant has just been questioning me, but it got so boring that I ran away and crawled in among your envelopes. What sort of silly machine is that?'

Miss Niven could only manage: "Heh? What?"

"The letters look so peculiar," said Virgil, reading out what he saw on the typewriter keys: "QWERTYUIOP? What does 'Qwertyuiop' mean? Is it police language, or some nasty animal?"

Miss Niven searched through her bag, trying to

find a pill for her nerves. It always helped. She suffered from nerves a lot because of all the thieves and murderers and swindlers and con-men and muggers and burglars and vandals and terrorists who passed daily through her little room to be interrogated. So in fact she liked a dwarf much better.

"Gracious me," she said. "In among my envelopes!"

But Virgil cried: "I asked you what it means: Qwertyuiop."

"Oh, nothing," she said. "They are keys which you have to press and then the letters appear on the paper."

"Will you show me?" asked Virgil.

Miss Niven blushed. "I'm not allowed to talk to you," she said. "I shall have to warn the sergeant."

"Of course," said Virgil. "But do first show me what you mean."

She rolled a sheet of paper into the machine and typed Virgil's name in full, in capital letters: VIRGIL NOSEGAY.

"How lovely, how lovely!" cried the dwarf. "You go and call the sergeant now. Just tell him I'm here."

Miss Niven left the room, went down the passage, and to the counter where Constables Stoker, German and Hill were busy.

"The sergeant," she said. "Isn't the sergeant here?"

"No," said the constables. "Somebody's just broken out. A prisoner. He's gone looking for him with the inspector and Fisher."

"I know!" cried Miss Niven. She ran on, through the swing door, across the lobby, through the revolving door and down the steps. There was the sergeant, peering along the road. The inspector had already reached the corner and PC Fisher was three streets away.

"Quick, quick!" called Miss Niven. "He's with me. The dwarf. He was among my envelopes."

"Well, really," said the sergeant, and he followed her back.

But there was no longer a dwarf in Miss Niven's little room. The sheet of paper on which she had been typing was still in the machine. VIRGIL NOSEGAY was written there in capital letters. But after it two more words had been added: WAS HERE. The sergeant read it aloud: "Virgil Nosegay was here."

The sergeant's neck, which was bent forward, very slowly turned red . . .

29 The Little Cushion

With his neck and his cheeks red with anger, the sergeant straightened up. "What does this mean?" he thundered.

But the inspector, who had also come in, remained calm. "It is quite clear," he said. "It simply means that the prisoner *was* here. In other words, he no longer *is* here." The inspector was right. Virgil was no fool. He had got Miss Niven to type his name and watched carefully how she did it. Then he had sent her off to fetch the sergeant and the inspector and quickly, quickly, he had typed the words WAS HERE after his own name, banging the keys down with his fists. Then he had jumped down from the desk to Miss Niven's chair – there was a soft little cushion on it – and then he had thrown the little cushion on the floor and jumped down on to it, and then . . .

"I say!" cried Miss Niven suddenly. "My little cushion is on the floor. Why is that, I wonder?"

"That too!" thundered the sergeant.

But the inspector remained calm. "Oh, come," he said. "It must have slid off when you got up."

"It's never happened before," she said.

But the sergeant shouted: "He'll be underneath it, that dwarf! Quick, quick!" He snatched up the metal wastepaper basket and put it upside down over the little cushion. "There! He won't escape again."

"No indeed," said the inspector. "But what now? How are we going to catch him now?"

Miss Niven began to sob. "Oh dearie, dearie me, that poor innocent little dwarf!

"Innocent?" cried the sergeant. "He incited dogs, and broke in and stole. He's a really suspicious character."

"Good Lord," said the inspector. "But what are we to *do?*"

"Fetch assistance," said the sergeant. He went to the passage and called: "Stoker, German, Hill! Come here!"

The three policemen who were sitting at the counter, busy sorting out parking tickets, rose slowly to their feet.

"Here we are, men!" said the sergeant, when they came into the room. "There is a prisoner under there." He pointed to the wastepaper basket.

The three constables looked at each other. "Very well, sergeant," they said.

"You must form a cordon," said the sergeant. "A closed cordon, with your feet, all round it. While I pick up the wastepaper basket."

"Very well, sergeant," they said again. They had got the message. Together with the inspector they formed a circle, a wall of feet, of high, black police shoes, polished till they shone, except for PC Hill's. He had forgotten again.

"Boohoo, boohoo!" went Miss Niven. "The poor little gnome."

But the sergeant said: "Silence!" And then he said: "One, two, three!" and picked up the waste-paper basket.

There lay the little cushion, just as before.

It's like a conjuring trick, thought Miss Niven to herself. She looked at the little cushion in the middle of the circle of policemen's feet, and she thought: just fancy if the little dwarf tied all the laces together now, ha ha, that would – and at the terribly exciting moment when the sergeant stooped to pick up the little cushion, Miss Niven began to bubble over with laughter.

The sergeant straightened up again. "Miss Niven," he said, in his dangerous hiss, "there is

nothing to laugh at here! Understood?"

He bent over again; the legs of the constables and the inspector wobbled with excitement (or with laughter?) and after a whispered one, two, three, the sergeant jerked the cushion away.

Underneath it was nothing. Nothing at all.

Where was Virgil?

I will tell you where Virgil was: on the counter, among all the parking tickets which the three constables had been sorting when they were called away. And now Virgil was sorting them. On every ticket he wrote the name of horrid Mr Walker from opposite, so that he should receive a hundred or more fines. "That mean old man!" muttered the dwarf. "Reporting me to the police! I'll pay him out!"

Then he jumped to the floor, without a soft little cushion, and walked down the passage. But after all that the heavy swing door was closed, and suddenly he heard a thunderous laugh from the constables in Miss Niven's little room. I'd better be off, thought the dwarf.

He ran back to the counter, because he had seen a door behind it which stood slightly ajar.

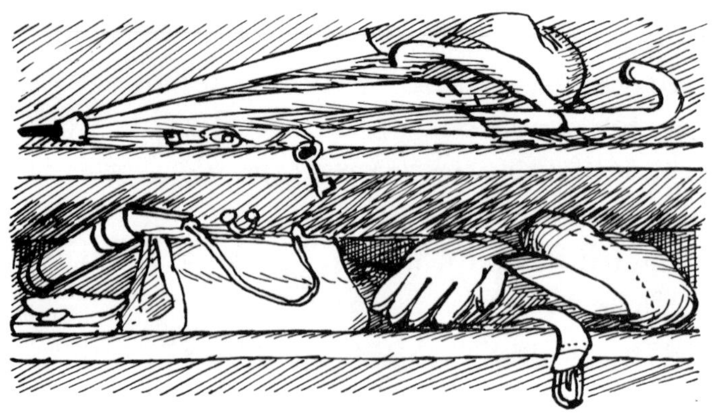

30 A Cupboardful

Virgil darted through the crack in the door behind the counter. Just in time, because the three policemen were coming back.

"If you ask me," they were grumbling to each other, "it's the sergeant who ought to be going to see the spikytwist. Tcha! A suspect under an upside-down wastepaper basket! Or was it just his little joke?"

They went dozily back to work on their parking tickets. Virgil, meanwhile, had been hoping that the door would lead him to another passage and perhaps to a back exit that he could slip through. But he was wrong. The door was a cupboard door and now he was really trapped.

It was a very big cupboard with a lot of shelves and the shelves were covered with – good heavens, what were all these things? Hats, scarves, keys, umbrellas, jackets, purses, jerseys, dog-leads, anoraks, gloves, bags, caps, wallets, watches, files, transistors, books, a helmet, a fishing-rod, gold rings, bracelets, one left shoe, two knives, eleven socks . . . Virgil could not see more than these because suddenly the cupboard was pitch-dark. The crack through which the light had come in had gone and Virgil heard the lock turning, click-clack.

PC Hill had turned the key; he had once again forgotten to shut the cupboard door and now he was going to do it quickly before anyone noticed, so that he should not get into trouble. Hrm!

Fortunately the others were still busy talking about the joke. But when the sergeant came and said that, above all, all doors must be kept closed, including the swing door in the passage, they replied obediently: "We'll see to it, sergeant," and went on with their parking tickets.

"Well, well," said one after a time, "that Mr Walker is quite something. I've counted up to a hundred already."

Virgil could hear them from the cupboard and it made him laugh. There, he thought, it has worked. He nestled comfortably in a woolly scarf on one of the shelves and fell asleep. That was what he always did when he was stuck. 'When I wake up I'll think about it,' he thought.

But when Virgil woke up again he could still see nothing. The cupboard door was shut, all the doors throughout the police station were shut, and there was now a fat policeman sitting at the counter. He had relieved the other three for the night, because it was night time now.

And it was the voice of the fat policeman which

woke Virgil up. "What did you say, madam?" he heard.

There must have been someone at the counter, because now Virgil could hear a complaining voice: " . . . lost, officer," complained the voice, "yesterday I think. In Sheep Street. Or it may have been in Canterbury Lane. Or by the railway. A little dog-lead, you know. Green, with a bell on it. I think somebody may have found it and brought it here."

Virgil turned over crossly. He was just about to shout: "Who's that waking me up?" when suddenly he heard the fat policeman's voice close to him:

"We'll just have to look and see, madam, let's have a look in Lost Property, shall we?" and suddenly the cupboard door was wide open.

Virgil jumped up.

"Hey!" cried the fat policeman. "Just look here! I've got it!"

And he picked up a tinkling lead, green with little bells on it. "This one?"

The complaining lady burst into glad cries and the cupboard door closed again, click-clack.

Well now, thought Virgil. Lost property! So I'm here among the lost property, am I? He got up and began to scramble around the cupboard, feeling all the objects in the darkness.

"How strange people are," he murmured. "How could anyone lose their left shoe?" But that suddenly made him think of Jasper, who had lost his boots on the moor, and with whom the whole adventure had begun. "If Jasper could only lose his boots again," thought Virgil, "but somewhere where they could be found by someone else and brought here. Then they would be lost property too, and I could crawl inside until Jasper came to get them. That would be lovely!"

He crawled inside the left shoe for a minute to feel what it would be like and then he felt a hole in the sole and in the wooden floor under it. A mousehole!

There now, thought the dwarf. There is always a way out of everything. As long as you're not looking for it.

He wriggled through – it was an old mouse passage – and where did he finish up? Back in Miss Niven's little room, where the door was firmly closed.

I'm not going to get anywhere here, thought Virgil. But to make sure he took another look round the room. The light of a street lamp fell on Miss Niven's desk and on the typewriter.

And then Virgil had an idea . . .

31 Peter

Virgil had another good look at Miss Niven's desk and then he went slowly towards it. "It's worth trying," he muttered to himself.

Once again Miss Niven had left the bottom drawer full of envelopes open. Virgil took one out and a sheet of writing paper as well, climbed, panting, up the chair and on to the desk, switched on the desk light and rolled the sheet of paper into the typewriter just as he had seen Miss Niven doing.

And then he began to type. Very slowly, searching for the letters. "D-e-a-r J-a-s-p-e-r."

It was a long letter. It took Virgil at least an hour to type. Then the envelope had to go into the machine, for the address. It was a real police envelope, with Police printed on the outside.

Virgil put the letter in the envelope, stuck it down, and put it in the tray which said "Outgoing Mail". He had watched Miss Niven doing all these things.

"Dear me, what a lot of work," sighed the dwarf,

"but there's nothing more for me to do until I'm safe at home. I'll have a nice comfy sleep."

Once again he jumped down to the floor via the chair with the soft little cushion, crawled back along the mouse tunnel to the Lost Property cupboard, rolled himself up in the soft scarf and fell asleep.

Next morning Miss Niven saw the letter in the tray. She thought it was a letter from the sergeant. "Oh gracious," she murmured, "they must have forgotten to take this to the post yesterday!"

She quickly did it herself before anyone had noticed and sent it Express to make sure.

That afternoon the letter reached Jasper's house.

"From the police!" he said, startled. "It will be about Virgil of course. But why has it got my name on it?"

Jasper tore the envelope open and began to read: "Dear Jasper. Listen, you've got to . . ."

Jasper read the letter. "What?" he said.

Then he read the letter again. "Oooh!" he shouted. "Now I've got it. Aaah!"

Then he ran upstairs and a moment later he was running down again with a plastic bag swinging on his arm. He ran out through the kitchen, got his bike from the shed and pedalled away.

At the police station Constables Stoker, German and Hill were once again spending all day at the counter with their parking tickets.

"Well, well," said PC Hill. "That Mr Walker has parked his car in the wrong place one hundred and twenty-seven times! How could that be, more than ten times a day!" The policeman was just going to check up and find out how such a thing could have happened, when a panting boy came in, his cheeks bright red, carrying a plastic bag which he banged down on the counter with the information:

"Found".

"What did you say, boy?"

"I found it," said the lad. "In the road. There are boots inside it."

"Well? And you brought it in?"

"Yes," said the boy. "It's for the Lost Property."

PC Hill opened the bag and looked at the boots. He turned up his nose. "Well," he said, "they're not worth much!"

"They are!" cried the boy. "They're only . . . er, I mean they're worth a whole lot."

"What's your name?" the policeman asked.

"Er, Peter," said the boy, turning even redder.

Then one of the other policemen called out: "Look, Hill, hurry up a bit. Chuck them in the cupboard and get on with your parking tickets."

PC Hill obeyed. While the boy ran off at high speed, the policeman put the boots in the cupboard.

Virgil went on sleeping soundly.

"Funny boy, that," PC Hill muttered to himself. "Peter. I don't believe his name was Peter."

Sighing, he returned to his parking tickets.

"And that Mr Walker," he grumbled on, "with his hundred and twenty-seven parking offences. I don't believe that, either."

And then PC Hill muttered a third time: "And as for someone coming to collect those boots that Peter handed in – I don't believe that at all."

32 The Boots are Found

Virgil was still sleeping, rolled up like a puppy, in the warm scarf in the Lost Property cupboard. It was night-time now, and once again the fat policeman was at the counter instead of the three who worked there by day.

Then a gentleman walked into the police station. "Tell me, constable," he said, "has a scarf been found? I've lost mine."

"Scarf," said the constable. "What colour?"

"Well, grey," said the man. "Grey stripes, with a bit of blue."

"Grey stripes with a bit of blue," repeated the fat policeman. "I'll have a look."

He opened the cupboard door and began to search through the jerseys and purses and leads and caps and bags and . . . yes, there was the scarf.

"Well, sir," he said, "there is a scarf here with grey stripes and a bit of blue, but there is a gnome on it as well."

"A gnome?" said the man. "No."

"Then I'm sorry, sir, but the scarf is not yours." The policeman was about to shut the cupboard door, but the man said: "Could I just have a look at it?"

The fat policeman shrugged his shoulders. "I don't mind," he said, and turning back he took the scarf off the shelf. "Here you are."

The man looked at it. "Gnome?" he said. "What's this about a gnome? There's no gnome anywhere on this scarf. What made you think of gnomes?" He sounded cross. "It's *my* scarf. Grey stripes with blue. Just as I said. And that's enough about gnomes. You'd better go and see an oculist."

The constable blinked. "But I saw it quite distinctly," he said.

And of course the policeman had seen a gnome. But it was not attached to the scarf: it was Virgil himself, wrapped up inside it. Virgil, who had woken up just in time to jump out of the scarf and crawl behind a hat.

"Can't a dwarf be left to sleep in peace anywhere?" he grumbled, and then, by the light that was still shining in through the half-open door, he saw the boots. Jasper's boots.

"Already," thought Virgil. "I didn't even notice them being brought in. He did that very quickly. Hurrah for Jasper!"

"He climbed into the right boot.

"Well, well," he mumbled on, "it still smells exactly the same as it did when the whole adventure began."

At home in Jasper's house, too, everything was the same as it had been when the adventure began.

"Silly, silly boy," cried his mother. "Losing your boots – and for the second time, too! Your lovely, expensive boots. What have you done with them now?"

"I, I . . ." Jasper stammered. "Virgil . . ."

"Virgil?" cried his mother. "What has he got to do with it? Virgil is at the police station."

"Yes!" cried Jasper. "That's why – the letter – I must go there!"

"You're not going anywhere!" cried Jasper's father. "You're staying in all evening!"

"But Virgil!" Jasper cried again.

"Virgil will come back on his own. He said so himself, so it will happen. You know that."

"Yes!" Jasper shouted desperately. "That's just it! My boots are . . ."

Father's mind was made up. "If you say *boots* once more . . .! Go to your room."

Jasper went. But once more, just as at the beginning of the adventure, late that night he slipped softly downstairs, out through the kitchen door, got his bike from the shed and rode off.

The fat policeman was dozing behind the counter and started when yet another member of the public came in.

"Hallo, lad. What are you up to at this hour of night? Have you run away from home?"

"Yes, no, sir," said the boy. "I . . . I wanted my boots. I mean, I've lost my boots. Red wellington boots, sir. Has anyone found them?"

"Red wellingtons? This late at night? I don't think so."

"Oh yes!" said the boy. "I . . . I mean: would you just have a look? They're in the cupboard."

The policeman looked at the boy. "How do you know?" he asked.

And the boy said: "It's written up there: Lost Property – on the door!"

"Ahem," said the fat policeman.

He opened the cupboard door, searched among the lost property and brought out a pair of red wellington boots. "These?"

The boy nodded.

"There!" said the policeman. "Now you'd better give me your name."

"Jasper," came a voice.

But it did not come from the mouth of the little boy. It came from the right boot . . .

33 The Ventriloquist

"Jasper!" came once again from the right boot.

The constable slowly put his head on one side. He looked from the boot to the boy, to the boot and back to the boy again. "Are you a ventriloquist?" he asked.

"Yeees!" cried the boot.

The constable looked at the boy again. "Your mouth is not moving at all," he said.

"Of course it's not!" cried the boot.

The policeman had been watching sharply. "Well, well! You're a real artist!" he told the boy. "How do you do it?"

"The secret of the boot!" cried the boot.

Then the boy said in his own voice: "Do be quiet Virgil, you silly thing!"

That made the policeman roar with laughter. "Virgil!" he cried. "Have your boots got names? The right one's called Virgil, is it? What's the left one called?"

"Oh er . . . er," stuttered the boy. 'The left one is called John."

"John?"

"Yes, John."

"Well! And can you make John talk, too?"

"No!" said the boy. "No. Can I have them now? I must go home."

"Here you are," said the policeman. "Here's John. And here's Virgil."

He put them on the counter. "I say! It feels as if Virgil is heavier than John."

"Oh no!" cried the right boot. "It only feels like that."

The little boy grabbed the boots and rushed away with them. And that was how Virgil passed – by boot – along the passage, through the swing door, across the lobby, through the front door, down the steps, and out of the police station, at last, at last.

They heard nothing of the escaped prisoner at the police station: neither the sergeant, nor the inspector, nor PC Fisher, nor Miss Niven, nor Constables Stoker, German and Hill. For all of them the case remained unsolved.

But not for Jasper.

He raced home, put his bike back in the shed, crept up to his room and shook out the boot on his bed. Just as he had at the beginning of the story, Virgil came rolling out.

"Fathead!" cried Jasper. "Donkey, dunce, twit, stupid, owl!"

"What now?" asked the dwarf.

"Talking out loud down there! The policeman

nearly found you!"

"So?" said Virgil. "I always get out of everything, don't I? I'm here now, aren't I?"

"Yes," said Jasper. "Yes. You're back. And that – well, that's fine."

"Yes," said Virgil. "And I almost overslept in the cupboard. You understood my letter perfectly, but I hadn't realized that you would come so quickly."

"Oh no?" said Jasper. "Did you think . . ."

But then the door of his room opened. His father came in. His mother came in. And Cathy too.

"What are these voices I can hear in the middle of the night?" asked father.

And mother said: "My boy, how did your boots suddenly come back?"

But Cathy cried: "Virgil! Virgil is back! Hurrah!"

They had a very late night. Virgil had to tell them all about the police station. And Jasper had to confess that he had taken his boots to the police station himself, under the name of Peter, who had found them somethere, and that he had later collected them, as Jasper, with Virgil inside.

"Yes," said Virgil. "I didn't want to walk all that way back. And I was lying comfortably in a scarf in that cupboard."

"Oh yes?" asked Cathy. "As comfortably as in my ballet shoes?"

"No," said Virgil. "Of course not."

"Are you coming back to sleep in my room tonight?" asked Cathy.

"No, mine!" cried Jasper.

Virgil said: "One week with one and one week

with the other."

He was going to stay with the family for two more weeks. Then it would be summertime, and he wanted to return to his friends on the moor.

When the two weeks were over Jasper took him back, on his bicycle.

The neighbour's dog Cinders barked goodbye, but Mr Walker from opposite was complaining bitterly to a policeman at his door. "One hundred and twenty-seven summonses?" he shouted. "What's this? Parking tickets? Good heavens, I haven't even got a car!"

Jasper and Virgil laughed all the the way to the moor.

But when Jasper put the dwarf down under the rowan bush they were not laughing.

"Goodbye!" said Virgil.

"'Bye," said Jasper.

He picked up his bike. When he looked round again, the dwarf had gone.